Other Series by Harper Lin

The Patisserie Mysteries

The Emma Wild Holiday Mysteries

The Wonder Cats Mysteries

The Pink Cupcake Mysteries

www.HarperLin.com

Cappuccinos, Cupcakes, and a Corpse

A Cape Bay Café Mystery Book 1

Harper Lin

ISBN-13: 978-1987859126
ISBN-10: 198785912X

Contents

Chapter 1	7
Chapter 2	22
Chapter 3	37
Chapter 4	54
Chapter 5	65
Chapter 6	81
Chapter 7	93
Chapter 8	106
Chapter 9	120
Chapter 10	130
Chapter 11	139
Chapter 12	154
Chapter 13	166
Chapter 14	180
Chapter 15	195
Chapter 16	205
Chapter 17	217
Chapter 18	226
Chapter 19	236
Chapter 20	245
Chapter 21	254
Chapter 22	266
Recipe 1: Dark Chocolate Cupcakes with Peanut Butter Filling	275
Recipe 2: Snickerdoodle Cupcakes	278
About the Author	287

Chapter One

I was bent over a cappuccino, carefully moving my milk pitcher to etch a design into the foam, when Mrs. D'Angelo burst into the café.

"Francesca!" she exclaimed so loudly that I jumped, pouring milk across the center of my design and out onto the saucer and counter.

I sighed and put down the milk pitcher, then plastered on a huge smile before looking up at her. "Mrs. D'Angelo!" I tried to sound happy despite having ruined my almost-finished cappuccino.

"Francesca!" she said again, coming around the counter. She grabbed my hands. "How *are* you, dear? Oh, you poor thing! I've been so worried about you!" She put one hand on my cheek, still managing to grasp both of mine in her other hand. She was exceptionally strong for an older woman. "You precious dear!"

I tried to keep the happy look on my face as I took half a step back, but some glimmer of distress must have flickered through my eyes because Mrs. D'Angelo pulled me into a tight hug.

"No, no, no, you dear girl, you come here!" She held me in such a way that my hands were pinned up by my shoulders, as if I had been raising them in surrender when she moved in.

I patted the woman's shoulders feebly with the slight range of motion I had in my wrists.

"You don't have to be strong, Francesca! You don't have to be strong!" she murmured.

At that moment, I wished I was strong—strong enough to break away from her grip. I caught the eye of one of my employees coming out of the backroom and sent her a "help me!" message with my eyes.

"Mrs. D'Angelo? Is that you?" Sammy asked, putting her hand lightly on Mrs. D'Angelo's back.

Mrs. D'Angelo mercifully let me go and turned her fountain of emotion in Sammy's direction. "Oh, Samantha!" She put one hand on Sammy's upper arm and her left one gripped mine. Her long red fingernails dug enthusiastically into our flesh. She looked between the two of us. "Samantha, I'm so glad Francesca here has you to help her through this difficult time. She needs good friends like you now more than ever." She rubbed my arm as she spoke, a welcome relief from her talon-like grasp.

"I'm doing all I can to help her out." Sammy smiled at the older woman.

"I'm sure you are, dear," Mrs. D'Angelo cooed. She turned back to me. "Do you need anything else? If there's anything you need, you know you can come to me or to any of us in the Ladies Auxiliary, and we'll do absolutely whatever we can to help you. We owe it to your dear mother's memory, God rest her soul, to help her dear Francesca." Mrs. D'Angelo crossed herself reflexively as she referred to my mother, releasing Sammy in the process.

Sammy took advantage of the freedom and stepped quickly over to the register, where customers were getting impatient, leaving me to deal with Mrs. D'Angelo and her monologue and grasping hands. I gave Sammy a look, and she smiled at me. She'd hear about it later, that was for sure. But for now, she was the lucky one getting back to work.

Out of the corner of my eye, I saw the tourist whose cappuccino I had been working on when Mrs. D'Angelo rushed in, impatiently tapping his fingers on the marble-topped table where he was sitting.

I looked helplessly at him then back at his cappuccino. "Mrs. D'Angelo—"

"Now, now, dear," she went on, oblivious to the fact that I was trying to escape. "No objections. None of us would have it any other way. Anything for our dear Carmella's daughter. Now, what time is it?" She looked at her watch. "Oh, heavens, I didn't even realize! I'm due at the library for our Genealogy Society meeting! I have to run!" She hurried back around the counter toward the door. "Now, don't forget what I said, Francesca dear! Anything you need!" And she was gone, in as much of a whirlwind as she'd arrived, leaving only a cloud of her floral perfume and some red fingernail prints in our arms.

I sighed as I began a fresh cappuccino for the man who was still waiting impatiently for his drink. Not that I could blame him.

"I need a nap after that!" I whispered to Sammy as we moved around each other in the small drink prep area. "That woman has more energy in her seventies than I've had in my entire life!"

Sammy giggled. "I think she gets it from exhausting other people."

I bent over the steaming cappuccino, carefully crafting a rose in the foam. I tried not to rush, but I could feel the man's eyes boring into the top of my skull as I worked. I finally put down the milk pitcher and stood back to assess my handiwork. Certainly not my best, but it was still better than a person could find anywhere else in town, or in most places on the Massachusetts coast.

I picked up the mug and saucer and carefully walked them around the counter to the man who had ordered the drink. I set it gently on the table in front of him, positioned perfectly so he'd have the best view of my creation. "So sorry about the wait, sir. My apologies." I gave him my very best café-owner smile.

"I hope it don't always take this long," he grunted. He took a drink without even glancing at the rose I'd crafted.

I smiled sweetly. "I really am very sorry, sir." *Rude.* I turned to go back around the counter. *I should have known that when I saw the Yankees jersey.*

Despite living in New York City for years before moving back home, I've always been a Massachusetts girl at heart, and during baseball season, I bleed Boston Red Sox red. Well, I suppose everyone bleeds red, but that just shows how much better the Red Sox are than our rivals to the south. No one *literally* bleeds Yankee blue.

I took up my post in front of the espresso machine, wiping things down while I waited for the next order.

Sammy worked the cash register and called out the next drinks to make just seconds later. "I need two lattes, please!"

I set about making the drinks, brainstorming what I would design in their foam as I worked. I steamed the milk for the first drink, getting it about halfway finished before I pulled the espresso. The timing had to be perfect or the espresso would get bitter. Fortunately, I'd been making cappuccinos since I could see over the counter, so it was second nature to me. I decided on coordinating sun and starburst patterns. I made the sun design first, pouring the center circle of foam then using a toothpick to draw out the rays. Finishing that, I moved on to the starburst.

Work, except for Mrs. D'Angelo's interruption, was a cherished distraction from the circumstances that had brought me back to my hometown on the Massachusetts coast. This café had been in my family for three generations. First it had belonged to my grandparents, who opened it shortly after arriving from Italy almost seventy years ago. My mother grew up here, making coffee and cannoli alongside her parents. It was her sanctuary when her marriage fell apart and she needed a way to support herself and her young daughter. Now it's my sanctuary.

Like a lot of people who grew up in this town, I left for college and didn't come back. Not for a long time, anyway. I went to school in Boston and got a job working in public relations in New York. The hours were long, and the competition was fierce.

I was happy at first, but it wore on me over time. I managed to carve out a personal life in what little free time I had, dating then getting engaged to a guy I thought was the man of my dreams. *Thought* being the key word.

He broke my heart, removing his things from the apartment we shared, the apartment I couldn't afford on my own, and running off with a girl from his office. I'd cried for days, pulling it together just enough to go to work, then coming home and crying some more while I packed up my own things so I could move into a new apartment when I found one. I spent hours on the phone with my mother.

"Francesca, come *home*," she'd say and tell me how the café had saved her when she'd been in my position so many years ago.

But I didn't listen. I stayed in New York to fight for what was left of my life.

And then my mother died.

I quit my job, broke my lease, and moved back to the Massachusetts coast. I buried my mother, moved into the house where my grandparents had raised my mother and me, and stepped back behind the counter at Antonia's Italian Café as if I had never left.

So there I was, two weeks later, back in the place where I had spent the better part of my thirty-four years, creating intricate designs in the artisan cappuccinos our café had always specialized in. It wasn't a terribly big place, just ten two-top tables along the exposed brick walls and ten oversized armchairs arranged in groups and nestled into cozy corners. All the tables and chairs were mismatched because my grandparents hadn't been able to afford coordinating furniture when they first opened the café. My grandmother had frequented estate sales and auctions, picking up one table or chair at a time until the space was full. They're pretty old, but my mother had maintained them by reupholstering any that needed rejuvenating. It was an eclectic mix, but it gave off a surprisingly cozy, homey feel.

Compared to Antonia's, the stylish coffee shops I'd visited in New York seemed sterile and severe. And of course the burnt dirt water they served and tried to call coffee was even worse than it sounded when compared to the drinks my family proudly made. Don't get me wrong, plenty of little family-owned diners in New York can make a great cup of coffee, but when you got into the espresso drinks the fancier places tried to serve, that was when you got bilge water. My grandparents would roll over in their graves if I ever even thought about bringing in pre-roasted beans, let alone pre-ground ones. That was part of the magic of Antonia's—we did everything, from start to finish. Our milk even came from local dairy farms.

Our coffee wasn't the only thing that kept people coming in. We served some food, mostly desserts and sandwiches, but it was really the way we catered to our customers that kept us busy. The café was popular with book clubs, partly because of our coffee, partly because of the comfortable chairs, and partly because we let them drag the tables and chairs around however they wanted. As long as they bought something and didn't violate fire code, we were more than happy to accommodate them. My mother had even encouraged them to place their orders ahead of time so we could have everything ready when they came in. Even without the book clubs, we stayed busy, especially during the summer tourist season.

I finished the second drink and passed them to Sammy to deliver to the customers' table. Finally, I got a moment to catch my breath.

As Mrs. D'Angelo had said, Sammy really had been a lifesaver since my arrival back in Cape Bay. She had worked alongside my mother for years—since Sammy was in high school actually—and she knew the café like the back of her hand. In my first few days back, she had helped me learn the new cash register, taught me the stocking and ordering procedures, and generally followed me to make sure I didn't make a mess of things. Now I relied on her the same way my mother had, working side-by-side to keep the café humming along smoothly. We had some part-time help from a couple of teenagers out of school for summer vacation, but the two of us, plus our two bakers, carried the bulk of the load, and it was going great. Except, of course, when someone came along and started talking about my mother. At those times, the reality and freshness of her death hit me, and focusing on my work became infinitely harder.

"I'm going to take a break," I told Sammy as she came back around the corner.

She looked at me, her eyebrows drawn together. "Are you okay?"

I usually took a lunch break and not much else, so this was unusual. "Yeah, I just need to get some air."

I pulled off the apron I wore to protect my sleek black clothing, which was the uniform of the New York City public relations world, as I stepped into the backroom. Outside, I took a deep breath. We were in town, but the tang of the salt air was still strong. It felt good in my lungs. It was the smell of my home and childhood. It made me happy to be back and nostalgic for what I had lost. I closed my eyes and leaned back against the café's brick wall. I must have been out there longer than I thought, because the next thing I knew, Sammy poked her head out the door.

"Francesca?" she called quietly.

"Hmm?" I murmured, my eyes still closed.

"Why don't you get out of here? You've been working nonstop since you got back. You deserve some time off."

I'd been in the café from open to close since the day after my mother's funeral, but that was the way I wanted it. If I stayed busy enough, I couldn't think. "I can't. I can't leave you here alone."

"I won't be alone. I already called Becky to come in. You need the rest."

I opened my eyes and looked at her. She had one hand on her hip and was holding the door open with the other. Wisps of her long blond hair had escaped the low ponytail she always wore at work and were swirling around her head in the breeze. Despite the golden halo effect her hair was giving her, she had a stern expression to go with her assertive posture. She didn't look as if she would take no for an answer. I sighed and looked at my watch. Three hours to close. Going home now wouldn't be the end of the world. I could make myself some dinner, take a long bath, maybe go to bed a little early. It would be a treat.

"Are you sure?" I asked.

"Yup. In fact"—she leaned to look around me at the parking lot on my other side—"I think I see Becky pulling up now." She waved at me. "So go on, get out of here."

I had to admit she was right. I sighed and pushed myself off the building. "Okay, you got me. I'll go home. Let me just get my purse."

Sammy patted my back as I walked past her. "You'll thank me for it tomorrow."

I fished my Italian leather purse out of the cabinet where we kept our personal belongings while we're working and slid it onto my shoulder. My mother and grandmother had never cared much for fashion or labels, but they had instilled a firm belief in Italian leather in me. Shoes, bags, belts, wallets—all leather goods had to be imported from Italy. Nothing else was good enough. Even after all my years in New York, surrounded by devotees of French red-soled Louboutins, I still swore by Ferragamo, Prada, Gucci, and Bottega Veneta.

I straightened a few boxes of supplies that weren't lined up properly on their shelves against the wall. Then I noticed that a couple of them were empty enough that their contents could be combined and the boxes thrown away, so I started cleaning them out.

"What are you doing?" Sammy asked.

"I'm just straightening things up a little bit. I don't want to leave everything all over the place for you to clean up tonight." I knew I was making excuses not to go home.

"Things are not a mess. Those boxes are fine the way they are, and they're certainly not something you need to take care of now!" Sammy took me by the shoulders and turned me toward the door that Becky was walking through.

"Hi, Francesca!" Becky said as she walked in.

"Hi—" I started.

"Francesca was just leaving," Sammy said, cutting me off. She guided me to the door and walked me outside. "Go! We have everything under control. The café will still be here for you to fuss over in the morning." She released my shoulders, walked back to the door, and kicked out the doorstop. "Bye now!" She waved.

The door thunked closed. I sighed, staring at it for a minute. There was no way Sammy would let me back in today, even if I did own the place. And a long, hot bath really did sound pretty good. I adjusted my purse on my shoulder and started on what I thought would be an uneventful walk home.

Chapter Two

It wasn't a long walk—just a few blocks. My grandmother had never learned to drive, so when she and my grandfather decided their family needed more space than was available in the apartment above the café, they needed to look close by. The house they found was a Cape Cod that was old even when they bought it. It was nestled among other Cape Cods on a street two blocks over and perpendicular to Main Street, where the café was. The previous owners had adapted the house so that it had one downstairs bedroom and two upstairs bedrooms—one for the boys and one for the girls, my grandparents thought. But no children came along, besides my mother, and the third bedroom stayed empty until I moved into it as a child.

I decided to take a shortcut across a few backyards, the same shortcut I used to take when I was a kid running back and forth between the house and the café ten times a day. I hadn't taken it since I'd been back because I'd still been wearing my New York stilettos, which weren't exactly suited to grassy wandering, but my aching feet had finally convinced me to dig some of my mother's loafers out of her closet. Fortunately, her obsession with Italian leather, combined with regular visits to Cape Bay's cobbler, meant that her nearly twenty-year-old shoes were still in great shape and comfortable to boot.

I turned off the sidewalk and stepped onto the grass. The shade from the trees was a nice break from the summer heat. With how humid Massachusetts summers could get, I had learned long ago to keep my thick mass of hair in a chignon pretty much the entire season. As a teenager, I had argued with my mother that black hair made me hotter in the summer sun and

I would be so much cooler if I could just dye it blond. She refused, insisting that it would turn orange. I didn't believe her and bleached it at a friend's house one summer day when I was avoiding working at the café. It turned orange. Very, very orange. After that, I listened to my mother's beauty advice.

I trekked across a few yards, reminiscing about all my childhood adventures. As I got close to my house, I saw Mr. Cardosi, the town barber, sitting on his back porch. He had lived two doors down from my grand-parents my entire life, and I had played and gone to school with his son Matteo, or Matty as I had always called him. It was unusual for Mr. Cardosi to be home at that time of day, but it was unusual for me to be home at that time of day too.

"Hello, Mr. Cardosi!" I called, waving.

Mr. Cardosi didn't move. I thought that was strange, but when he sat out back, he usually had his radio turned to the Red Sox game, so maybe he just couldn't hear me. I decided to wait until I was a little closer to call out again.

I waved again as I got into his backyard. "Hel–"

I stopped, noticing that Mr. Cardosi's chin was resting on his chest. Was he sleeping? I cut across his yard to check on him. This had always been the kind of neighborhood where everybody watched out for everybody else. I appreciated it now, but I'd hated it when I was a kid and Matty and I were running around, causing trouble. I'd never once made it home before the news of whatever mischief we'd gotten ourselves into had reached my grandmother's ears.

I walked across the lawn, wondering if I should call out to Mr. Cardosi so as not to startle him or stay quiet to let him keep sleeping. Not wanting to scare the old man and give him a heart attack, I called out again. "Mr. Cardosi! Mr. Cardosi!"

He didn't move. I slowed down as I got to the porch.

"Mr. Cardosi?" I said more quietly. Still nothing. I nudged his shoulder. "Mr. Cardosi?"

He slumped farther over, and I got a sick feeling in the pit of my stomach. Mr. Cardosi wasn't asleep—he was *dead*. I backed away slowly, reaching for my phone in my purse so I could call for help.

I lurked at a distance while I waited for the police and ambulance to arrive. I knew I couldn't leave, and really, I didn't want to just abandon poor Mr. Cardosi, but I didn't want to hover too closely either. I didn't know how he'd died, but I knew the police would want to look around, and I didn't want to mess with things. Besides, being so close to a dead body was a little unsettling.

I wasn't too surprised that the police car arrived first—it's a small town, and the police station is just across the street from the café. The ambulances have to come all the way from the next town over. I heard the cruiser pull up, and I poked my head around the house and waved. The officer climbed out of the car and approached the house. He was a big, imposing man. Not overweight, just very tall and broad.

"You the one who requested police?" he called when he spotted me.

"Yup, that's me!" I yelled.

He strolled a little bit closer then motioned me toward him. "How 'bout you come over this way for me?"

He sounded suspicious. His brow was furrowed as I walked toward him. He was clearly trying to figure out who I was and what I was doing there. While everyone pretty much knew everyone else in town during the off-season, the summer brought a lot of tourists, and the officer seemed to think I had wandered off the beach and into trouble. We recognized each other simultaneously.

"Mike!" I exclaimed.

"Francesca!" he said at the same time.

He held out his arms, and I hurried to give him a hug. Mike was another former classmate of mine. It wasn't really surprising to run into him, but it was pleasant all the same. I hadn't seen him since I'd gotten back.

He held me out at arm's length. "You look great!" Then a shadow passed over his face. I knew he'd remembered why I'd moved back. "I'm really sorry about your mom. She was such a great lady. Sandy and I would have come to the funeral, but we had booked a trip to Disney with the kids..." He seemed to realize how awkward it was to go from talking about my mother's death to his trip to Disney. He grimaced and looked at his shiny cop shoes.

"It's fine, Mike, really. You have your life to live."

Mike smiled, grateful for the out. "So I heard you're sticking around for a while?"

"That's the plan. I was kind of in a rut in New York, and I figured coming home would be a good change of pace."

"That's great! That's really great. We're happy to have you back in town." He chuckled. "I'm sure you'll see it hasn't really changed all that much over the years."

I laughed with him. "I've noticed! It's like stepping right back into high school! All the old neighbors are living in the same places–"

All of a sudden, I remembered the neighbor who had prompted the call that had brought Mike out here. The look on Mike's face told me he had just remembered too. He rubbed a hand back and forth across his high-and-tight hair.

"So, uh, you were concerned about Mr. Cardosi?" he asked.

I nodded. "Yeah, I was walking home, and I took the old shortcut through the back. When I was coming across the yard, I yelled to say hello, but he didn't move, so I went over to check on him, and, well..." I gestured toward the back of the house.

"He's around back?" Mike asked, starting in that direction.

"On the patio."

Mike took a wide path toward the back of the house, I guessed so he could get a good look before he got close. When he got to where he could see Mr. Cardosi sitting in his lawn chair, he held a hand out to me, motioning for me to stop. He glanced back. "You check his pulse or anything?"

I shook my head. "No. I just nudged him, and he—he kind of slumped."

Mike nodded and continued across the back of the house toward Mr. Cardosi. He rested his right hand on his gun. A cop habit, I assumed.

"Mr. Cardosi?" he called softly. He took a couple of steps closer. "Mr. Cardosi?"

There was no movement from the lawn chair. Mike reached out a hand toward Mr. Cardosi's neck and held it there for a moment, checking his pulse. He withdrew his hand and pushed the button on the walkie-talkie on his shoulder.

He spoke quietly, but I could just hear, "You can let the ambulance know there's no rush. He's gone."

Hearing that, I realized I'd been holding out some hope that Mr. Cardosi really was just sleeping very soundly, or maybe even had passed out. Not something I'd normally wish for, but given the options, I would have preferred it.

Mike walked a wide circle around Mr. Cardosi's chair, leaning down to look from all angles. I wondered if that was standard procedure or if he'd seen something suspicious. I hadn't noticed anything, but I also hadn't lingered once I'd realized the situation. Mike walked back toward me with a grim expression. I felt tears unexpectedly fill my eyes. So much had happened in my life recently, and this was just one more thing on top of it all.

Mike must have noticed my expression because he put his hand awkwardly on my shoulder. "I'm sorry, Francesca. I know you knew him well growing up."

I sniffled. "It's not just that. Everything has changed so much lately..." I covered my face with my hands. "Sammy made me leave early today because she thought I needed a break and now—" I waved toward Mr. Cardosi.

Mike patted my shoulder. "It's a lot." He seemed very uncomfortable.

I took a couple of deep breaths then shook my shoulders. It was what I always did when I was trying to cheer myself up—literally shake the bad feelings off me. I wiped my eyes and forced a smile. "Whew—sorry about that. Just got a little overwhelmed there for a minute."

"That's all right." He seemed happier now that I had regained my composure. "Now, uh, I know you told me you were taking a shortcut home. Is this a way you come often?"

I shrugged. "Kind of. I mean, it's the way I always walked to and from the café growing up, but I think I've only done it once or twice since I got back in town."

"Uh-huh." Mike reached in his breast pocket and pulled out a small notebook with a pencil through the spiral at the top. "And is this the time of day you usually come home?"

"No," I said. He must not have heard me say that Sammy had sent me home early. "Usually I stay until close at eight, but today—" I thought about telling him about Mrs. D'Angelo's visit but decided against it. "Today, Sammy thought I should leave early and get some rest." I paused while he scribbled, then I thought of something.

"Wait, why? Did you see something? You don't think someone–" Crime was virtually nonexistent in Cape Bay, and murder was practically unheard of. Surely he didn't think someone had killed Mr. Cardosi!

Mike looked up from his notebook and smiled at me. "Just trying to make sure I have all the details right for my report." He resumed writing, looking at me again when he was finished. "Now did you see anybody nearby? Anybody coming or going? Anything suspicious?"

I shook my head. "There were a couple of tourists out on the street when I left the café, but once I got on the side streets, I didn't see anyone."

Mike grunted and wrote something else. "Sammy can confirm what time you left the café?"

"Yes, and Becky had just gotten there. Mike, you're not telling me something. You don't think I did something to him, do you?"

Mike smiled at me again. It wasn't the friendly smile from when he first recognized me. It was more of a cop-placating-a-citizen smile. "No, I don't. I'm just establishing a timeline so they know what they're working with when they do the autopsy." He waved toward Mr. Cardosi. "Case like this—no one around, no obvious cause of death—they always do an autopsy, just to figure out what happened."

I nodded. That sounded reasonable. Still, Mike's tone made me a little anxious, as if he wasn't quite telling me the whole truth.

"Helps the family rest a little easier too," he said.

The family! I remembered Matty. Poor Matty! His mother had died when we were kids, and now his dad was gone too. He'd be all alone in the world. *Like me.* I brushed the thought away. This wasn't about me, and I'd already had my breakdown for the day.

"Do you know if anyone's called Matty?" I asked.

"No, they haven't," he replied quickly. "Not unless one of the neighbors has seen my car out front and called him. Which is actually pretty likely."

It was. In a neighborhood where everybody watches out for everybody else, something like a police car parked out front was unusual enough to raise interest.

"Should I call him?" I reached for my phone that I'd shoved in my pocket. "I'm not sure if I have his number. Do you have it?"

Mike held out a hand. "No, no. I'll call him in a bit. Just want to finish getting some things down." He looked at his notepad. "When you left for work this morning, did you take the shortcut or go another way?"

I sighed. All his questions about my day were a little frustrating. "I took the main road. Out the front, down York Street, and out onto Main."

"What time was that?"

"About seven."

"And did you see Mr. Cardosi?"

I sighed again. All I wanted to do was get out of there. "This morning? No, I didn't."

"When was the last time you saw him?"

"A couple days ago. Maybe more. He was out getting the paper when I was on my way to work."

"And you haven't been around the back since that time?"

"You don't think he's been dead that long, do you?" I exclaimed.

Mike smiled his vaguely patronizing smile again. "Just asking questions."

"A lot of them!"

He chuckled. "Just doing my job. Now, have you been around the back since then?"

"No, no, I haven't."

"Have you seen Matt since then?"

"Matty? No, I haven't seen him since the funeral."

Mike looked at me sympathetically then back at his notebook. He seemed to be reading over what he had written. "I think that's about it." He flipped it closed then flipped it back open almost immediately. "Almost forgot—what's your cell phone number? That'd be the best way to reach you, right?"

"My cell or the café," I said before rattling off both numbers.

He jotted them down and flipped the notebook closed again, then he slid it back into his breast pocket. "Thanks for your help, Francesca." He looked toward the street. "Ambulance is sure taking its time, isn't it?"

It did seem as if it had been forever since I'd called. Just then, we saw the ambulance coming down the street, and at the same time, from the other direction, a car pulled up to the curb. The driver hesitated a moment then opened the door. Flying toward us with a panicked look on his face was Matty Cardosi.

Chapter Three

"Matty!" I shouted, stepping toward him.

He didn't even hesitate, just kept running toward where we were standing at the back of the house.

Mike, in full cop mode, walked forward to intercept him. "Matt!" He caught Matty as he tried to run by and held him in place.

"What's going on? Where's my dad? Let me go! Tell me what's going on!" Matty fought against Mike's grip, but Mike held on.

"Matt, Matt, you gotta calm down, man," Mike said as he struggled to keep Matty from running past him.

Matty made a few more attempts to escape before he gave up. "Okay, okay." He raised his hands in surrender, and Mike let him go slowly. Matty ran a hand through his hair. "What's going on? Where's my dad?"

I didn't know whether to reach out and comfort Matty from the pain I knew was coming or keep my distance. I ended up stepping closer so that I was barely an arm's length away, close enough to reach out and touch him but far enough away that I wasn't crowding them. It had been less than a month since I'd gotten the news about my mother that Matty was about to get about his dad, and I knew how much it hurt.

Mike took a deep breath. "Matt, I'm really sorry to have to tell you this—"

Matty stepped back, shaking his head rapidly. "No, no, no, no."

Mike stepped toward him and rested a hand on Matty's shoulder. "Matt, your dad passed away."

"But—he can't—" Matty glanced at me.

My eyes filled with tears I struggled to keep from pouring down my face.

"No, no, no," he repeated and ran around Mike.

Mike caught him as Matty got around the corner of the house to where he could see his dad slumped in his chair on the patio.

"Dad," Matty cried out as he collapsed to his knees.

Mike grasped Matty's shoulder. "You can't go over there, Matt. We have to process the scene."

"'Process the scene'?" Matty exclaimed. "What do you mean, 'process the scene'? Did someone kill my dad?" He looked frantically toward his dad's body as if he were searching for blood or bullet holes or some other sign of foul play.

"We don't know," Mike said. "In cases of unexpected deaths, we need to make sure we document everything just in case."

Matty sat back on his heels. Mike looked at me and nodded toward Matty. I knelt beside Matty and took his hand.

"They're just covering their bases, Matty," I said quietly.

Matty looked at me as if he were just noticing that I was there. "Franny," he said quietly.

I smiled at him sadly. I hadn't heard anybody call me "Franny" in years. We heard motion behind us and turned to see the paramedics we'd forgotten about wheeling a stretcher across the lawn.

"Uh, Francesca, how about you take Matt inside?" Mike suggested.

I looked at Matty, and he nodded. We both stood, our knees wet from the damp grass. Still holding hands, united in our orphan sorrow, we started toward the front of the house.

"Try not to touch anything!" Mike called after us.

I glanced back and nodded as Matty's hand tightened on mine. The added reminder that someone may have killed his dad pained him.

Mike said to the paramedics as we passed them, "Let me get my camera out of my car, then you can take him."

Matty and I walked to the front door. I reached for the knob, but Matty shook his head.

"He always keeps it locked," he said, reaching in his pocket for his keys.

But my hand was already turning the knob. I looked at Matty and saw him crumple.

"I'll make sure to tell Mike," I said. I knew we both hoped that his dad had just forgotten to lock it this once. As painful as my mother's death was for me, I couldn't imagine how much worse it would be if someone had taken her from me deliberately.

I glanced around as we stepped inside the house. Nothing looked disturbed or out of place. Everything was as quiet and in its place as if Mr. Cardosi had just stepped out to run to the store. Matty and I sat on the sofa in the front room, where we'd sat many times to watch TV in the afternoons. His house was a mirror image of my own, with the master bedroom on the right of the entrance instead of the left. Unless they'd been remodeled, Capes were all pretty much the same.

We were quiet, neither of us feeling the need to put our pain into words. That was all I had wanted in my first days back in town—to sit quietly and think about my mother. I stole a few glances at Matty. I'd only seen him briefly on the day I got back then again at my mother's funeral. I wasn't in much of a state of mind to pay attention to how he looked either time. I could see that, despite the tension and anguish in his face, he had been aging well. He had grown his thick, dark hair longer than he wore it in high school, but it was still a preppy, business-like length. He still had the same warm brown eyes. Back in school, those eyes could make me melt. We'd never dated, but that hadn't stopped us from flirting, and he'd been an expert at using those big brown eyes for that.

I didn't know how long we sat there. After my mother died, I'd felt as though I'd barely sat down on the train in New York when we arrived in Boston, so we could have been on that couch for five minutes or two hours. Time passed differently when your life was falling apart. There was a quiet knock on the door before it opened. I popped up off the couch, ready to fend off any prying neighbors, but it was just Mike. I sat back down next to Matty, who was staring off into space.

"Just going to take a few pictures," Mike said, nodding at us.

I nodded back as Matty continued staring.

Mike stepped into the master bedroom, and I saw the flash from his camera as he moved around the room, taking pictures. He went up the stairs next, and I heard his heavy shoes moving around the floor above us. Matty glanced at the ceiling then looked back at the spot on the carpet he seemed focused on. I leaned back on the couch and crossed then uncrossed my legs.

Mike came down the stairs a few minutes later and nodded at us as he passed through the living room to the back rooms of the house. I heard the click of the camera and saw the flash as he took more pictures. He seemed to be spending more time in the kitchen than he had in the other rooms. Finally, he came back into the living room and took a couple of pictures before sitting on a chair across from us. Matty didn't look at him until Mike cleared his throat.

"Did you find anything?" Matty asked, his voice hoarse.

"There were no visible marks on the body," Mike said professionally.

I cringed at his reference to "the body." That body had been Matty's dad just hours earlier. At least I hoped it had only been hours.

"They'll want to do an autopsy. Standard procedure to determine cause of death."

Matty nodded.

"Nothing appears disturbed in the house," Mike said.

"Can you tell me if your dad drank coffee throughout the day or just in the morning?"

"He makes a pot in the morning," Matty said, forgetting to use the past tense. "He drinks most of it before he goes into the shop then takes a travel cup with the last of it." Matty wrinkled his forehead, looking more alert. "Did Dad make it into the shop this morning?"

Mike shook his head. "I don't know. We'll check on it. Would you normally hear if he didn't go in?"

Matty sank back on the couch, shrugging. "Who knows? Dad would get in a mood sometimes and just decide he wasn't opening the shop that day. I'd drive by and see it closed and freak out, but when I'd call to check on him, he'd say he just didn't feel like cutting hair that day." He shrugged again. "Who knows? You know how Dad could be."

Mike nodded as he scribbled in his notebook. I wasn't sure what recent events Matty was referring to, but I remembered that Mr. Cardosi could fly off the handle at perceived slights. I remembered one time when the paper boy had delivered the Boston paper but not the local one and Mr. Cardosi went on a tirade. He had been certain the paper boy had done it deliberately, that the editor of the local paper had told him not to deliver it, and that there must be something negative about Mr. Cardosi in that day's paper. My grandfather had taken him our copy of the paper to show him that there was nothing about Mr. Cardosi in it at all, but Mr. Cardosi just accused him of being a part of the plot against him. He'd looked suspiciously at my grandfather and the paper boy for months after that.

"Do you know if there was anyone who had a grudge against your dad? Who might want to hurt him?" Mike asked.

Matty scoffed. "My dad's enemies are more in his imagination than in real life."

"Any close friends? Girlfriends? Anyone your dad might have been close to? We probably won't need to talk to them, but it's good to go ahead and get it in the notes."

Matty shook his head. "No, I mean, there're the guys at the barbershop—the employees and the regulars—but I don't think he really socialized with anyone outside of work."

Mike nodded and scribbled. "When was the last time you talked to your dad?" He was starting in with the same questions he'd asked me.

Matty visibly crumpled. "A couple of days ago. I've been so busy. God, I wish I'd called him. I just—I just had no idea it was the last time I'd talk to him."

"Did you see him that day or just talk on the phone?"

"The phone. I haven't seen him since last weekend." Matty bent forward and put his head in his hands. "If only I'd known it was the last time. I would have hugged him, told him I loved him."

"Were you and your dad close?"

"As close as he was to anyone. He's not a real sociable guy. Wasn't." Matty caught himself referring to his dad as if he were still alive. "He *wasn't* a real sociable guy." As if using the past tense hurt him all over again, Matty made a choking sound and covered his face with his hands.

I rubbed Matty's shoulder. I suddenly realized how lucky I was that I'd spent the hours after I found out my mother was dead on a train instead of being questioned by the police.

"I'm sorry, Matt." Mike looked over the notes he'd been scribbling as he talked to Matty. "Just a couple more questions. Did your dad have a will?"

"Yeah, I think so. It'd be in the safe in his closet."

Mike looked up with his eyebrows raised. "There's a safe in the closet?"

"Yeah," Matty said. "You didn't see it?"

"I just took pictures of what was visible. I didn't open the closet." Matty started to stand, but Mike raised his hand for him to stop. "Whatever's there or not there isn't going to change while we're sitting here. Let's wrap this up, and then we'll go look."

Matty sank back onto the couch.

"What about life insurance?" Mike asked.

"Yes," Matty said. "He got it after my mom died, so I'd have something if anything happened to him. The paperwork should be in the safe too."

"You're the sole beneficiary of both of those?"

"Yeah." Silence fell for a few seconds, then Matty snapped his head up to look at Mike. "Wait, you don't think—"

Mike held up his hand again. "No! No, no, no! Just making sure I have all the information. Like I said, we probably won't need to use any of this, but it's better to go ahead and get it all now."

Matty nodded.

Mike looked between his notebook and us several times then made a face and took a breath. "So you, uh, you showed up here at the same time as the ambulance, Matt."

I looked at Mike sharply. Despite his denial seconds before, the way he was talking to Matty made me suspicious.

Matty either didn't notice or ignored it, nodding in response. "Yeah, I did."

"Were you just driving by?"

"No, Mrs. Howard across the street called me. She saw Franny hanging around, and I guess she called here and no one answered, so she called me. She saw you pull up while we were on the phone and told me to hurry."

"And where were you when you got the call?"

"I was in the car, on my way home from work."

"So you just drove over here instead," Mike said.

"Yeah."

Mike nodded and scribbled some more in his notebook. "I think that about wraps it up for me. What's the best number to reach you?"

Matty gave him his cell phone number.

Mike jotted it down then looked at us. "Okay, want to show me the safe?"

Matty nodded and pulled himself up off the couch. Mike followed him across the room, and I brought up the rear. I lingered in the doorway as Matty walked to his dad's closet and opened it. From where I stood, I could see that the safe was still closed. Mike pulled his camera back out and took a couple of pictures.

"Can you open it up for me?" Mike asked.

Matty knelt in front of the safe. He spun the dial a few times then popped it open. Mike leaned in to take a few more pictures, then he nodded at Matty. Matty reached in and pulled out a stack of papers.

"Everything there that you expect?" Mike asked.

Matty sat on the foot of the bed and flipped through the papers. "Yeah, I think so. I don't really know everything he kept in here, but here's the will—" He pulled out a stapled bundle of papers and set it next to him on the bed. "And here's the life insurance paperwork." He laid the single sheet of paper on top of the will. "Do you need to look through these?" He held the other papers out to Mike.

"No, just wanted to make sure nothing was missing." Mike glanced around the room. "Speaking of missing, do you see anything that's not where it's supposed to be?"

Matty looked around. "No, I don't think so."

"Okay, well, if you notice anything, just give me a call, okay?" Mike reached into his breast pocket and pulled out a business card that he handed to Matty. "One for you, too." Mike passed another one to me.

I looked it over then put it in my pocket with my phone. I saw Matty put his on top of his dad's will and life insurance policy.

"Unless there's anything either of you want to ask me..." Mike looked between the two of us.

I shook my head.

"Matt?" Mike asked.

Matty looked up as though he'd gotten lost in thought. "What? No."

"All right then, I'll be on my way. If either of you think of anything else–" Mike was interrupted by a loud rap on the front door before it swung open.

One of the paramedics stuck his head in. "Hey, uh, Mike, we're about wrapped up out here. Does he want to–"

Mike nodded, understanding what he was being asked. He turned to look at Matty. "Matt, would you like to see the body before they take it away?"

I saw Matty's face go pale. He sat frozen for several seconds.

"There's nothing–no visible–" Mike stumbled over his words.

"Yes," Matty croaked, standing. "I'd like to see him."

The paramedic pushed the door farther open and stepped back outside. Mike went out first, then Matty, then me. The stretcher was on the front walk, a body bag containing Mr. Cardosi's ample form strapped on top of it. I almost bumped into Matty when he hesitated on the front step. The paramedics were standing at a respectful distance, and Mike stepped onto the grass so Matty would have room to walk by. Several of the busybodies who populated the neighborhood were gathered in front of Mrs. Howard's house across the street, gawking.

"You can do it, Matty," I whispered.

He glanced over his shoulder at me, nodded, and gave me the slightest of smiles. He stepped down the two front stairs and strode down the sidewalk to the stretcher. He stopped about a yard away, took a deep breath, and walked the remaining steps forward. I stayed at the bottom of the steps, not wanting to crowd Matty. He looked at his father's face, the only part of him not zipped up in the body bag, for a few minutes then stepped back and nodded to the paramedics. They walked forward, zipped the bag up the rest of the way, and wheeled Mr. Cardosi to the ambulance.

They slid the stretcher into the ambulance, closed the doors, got in, and drove away as we all watched in silence.

Mike shuffled his feet as Matty stood perfectly still on the sidewalk. Mike glanced at me then at Matty.

I walked forward and put my hand on Matty's shoulder. "Come on. Let's go inside."

Chapter Four

Before we could even turn around to go into the house, the neighborhood busybody contingent flocked across the street, past Mike on his way to his car, and surrounded Matty and me.

"Matteo, what happened?" "Was your dad sick, Matty?" "Francesca, dear, how did you find him? You were just walking home?" "What a fortunate coincidence, you finding him! He could have been out there God knows how long if you hadn't happened along!" "What an unfortunate coincidence, what with your mother just passing!" "If you need any help going through his things,

Matteo, I'd be happy to help. You know, I've lived just down the street there since your parents first moved in, back before you were even born."

The women's voice overlapped and merged as they went on and on in their chattering and so-called condolences that all too frequently sounded more like thinly veiled insults and criticisms.

"Such a tragedy, losing both your parents. And you so young yet!" "You're all alone in the world now! Neither of your parents will be there to see you get married when you finally find the right girl!" "Oh, your children won't have any grandparents!"

At that point, I grabbed Matty's arm and pulled him through the crowd toward the front door of Mr. Cardosi's house.

"Didn't Mike want us to look through the house?" I asked loudly.

"I can help you!" one of the women called.

"No, no, we have it!" We were almost at the door.

"I know where everything belongs! I spent quite a bit of time with Gino!"

Matty and I whirled around. Matty had specifically said that his dad didn't really socialize, so I wanted to see who was claiming to be his close friend. It was Mrs. Collins, a widow who lived across the street and two houses down, directly across the street from my house. She was rather well known for her, well, let's just call them "exaggerations." I narrowed my eyes at her, telegraphing a "back off" message. She stopped in her tracks at the edge of the group of women. Without taking my eyes off her, I pushed Matty toward the front door. I backed through it after him then slammed it and locked it for good measure.

"Thanks for that," Matty said as I stalked to the back door to lock that too.

Satisfied that we would have no surprise or accidental visitors, I walked back to Matty. "They should be ashamed of themselves."

I glanced around and noticed the living room curtains were open. I didn't put it past a single one of those women to walk through the flower beds and stare in, so I pulled the curtains closed, glaring through the window at the lingering crowd before I did. I walked through the first floor and closed the rest of the curtains before circling back to Matty, who was still lurking in the entryway.

"That should keep them at least from being full-on Peeping Toms," I said.

Matty nodded and shoved his hands in his pockets as he looked around. "He's really gone, huh?"

The aggression I had felt toward the meddling neighbors vanished, and I was filled again with sympathy for Matty. I rubbed his upper arm with my hand. "I'm so sorry."

He was quiet, staring at his shoes, then he looked at me. "So you found him?"

I swallowed hard and stepped back, shoving my hands deep in my pockets. "Yeah," I said as I nodded.

"Did he look–? How did he–?"

"I thought he was asleep," I said softly, understanding what Matty was asking.

"And you didn't see any–"

"No."

Matty nodded and looked at the ceiling with a sigh. "Thank you."

"For what?" I scoffed. I'd found his father's dead body and called the police. That was nothing special. In fact, I wouldn't have blamed Matty if he'd been angry with me.

"Finding him, calling the police, saving me from the biddy brigade out there," he listed.

"I didn't do anything special."

"Who knows how long he would have been back there if you hadn't walked by?"

I shrugged. "I'm sure it wouldn't have been long."

"Doesn't matter," Matty said. "Any time is too long."

I nodded sympathetically. My mother had collapsed in public and been whisked straight to the hospital. I couldn't imagine how awful it would be to know that your loved one had been lying somewhere, dead, for an extended period of time.

Matty took another deep breath. "Should we look around? See if there's anything missing or out of place that Mike didn't notice?"

"We?" I asked, surprised. We'd been close growing up, but I had barely seen Matty since high school. Even though I'd been thrust back into his life, I didn't expect him to want to share such a personal moment with me.

He shrugged. "I don't really want to be alone. And you've just been through the same thing. You're not going to be all nosey and stuff, asking me a bunch of intrusive questions about how I *feel* about everything."

Well, that was true. The first days after I'd been home, several of my mother's "friends" had come by, including some of the women from Mrs. D'Angelo's Ladies Auxiliary. They supposedly wanted to express their condolences, but they'd seemed more interested in poking around the house, making snide comments and asking not-so-subtly about what had gone wrong with my fiancé. The people who came by and just wanted to express their condolences and sit quietly with me, drinking a cup of coffee while I stared into space, were few and far between, but they were much more what I needed as I struggled to process everything.

"Okay then," I said. "Where do you want to start?"

"Living room?" Matty suggested.

That seemed like as good a place as any, so we walked back to the room where we'd sat and waited for Mike what seemed like ages ago, even though it had only been an hour. We worked our way through the house, one room at a time. Matty looked around in each, surveying the contents. He told me stories about the objects in each room—souvenirs they'd picked up on vacation, the lamp he'd broken when he threw a baseball through the open window while playing catch with his dad, knick-knacks that his grandparents had brought over from the old country, trinkets that had belonged to his mother. I already knew a lot of the stories from growing up with Matty, but I let him share them anyway. I knew how much he needed to talk about his dad without any pressure from me.

We finished without finding anything that looked unusual and returned to the living room.

"You want a cup of coffee?" Matty asked. "I know it's getting late, but I think my dad keeps some decaf. Although I feel a little inadequate making it for the coffee queen here."

I laughed a little. "Whatever you have will be fine." Yeah, I'd been around coffee my entire life and could tell a good cup from a bad cup by the look and the smell, but that didn't mean I didn't have manners. Besides, decaf or no, I knew I wouldn't be getting much sleep that night.

"All right," Matty said as we headed toward the kitchen. He reached to open the coffeepot to put in the filter and grounds but stopped suddenly.

"What is it?" I asked.

"I didn't notice before—the coffeepot's half full. It looks like Dad was only on his first cup." He pulled out the coffeepot and held it up for me to see.

Sure enough, it was only partially empty. Matty paused, staring at the coffeepot. The visual evidence of his dad's interrupted morning must have brought his grief back to the forefront. Not that I could blame him. He looked at it for a few more seconds then poured the coffee down the sink. He rinsed out the pot and started a fresh batch.

We sat in silence at the kitchen table, each of us lost in our thoughts of our own parent's recent passing. With a lot of people, that kind of silence might have been awkward, but with Matty, it felt completely comfortable. When the coffee was ready, Matty poured us each a cup and brought them back to the table.

"Sorry, no fancy designs," he said with a sad smile.

"It tastes just as good without them," I said before taking a sip. It did not taste good. Clearly Mr. Cardosi hadn't spent any more on his coffee than he'd absolutely had to. It was so bad, I actually wondered if there might be something wrong with the coffeemaker. I set my cup on the table. I'd had a lot of bad coffee in my life, and swallowed some of them down just to be polite, but I wasn't sure I could manage it with this one.

Matty put his cup down at the same time as I did. We sat for a moment, each staring at our cups.

"We can just throw it out if you want," he said.

I couldn't stop the laugh from bursting through my lips. Clearly Matty thought the coffee was just as bad as I did. "That might be a good idea," I said.

Matty took my mug and his cup over to the sink. He poured them both out then grabbed the pot from the coffeemaker and poured that coffee down the drain as well. He rinsed them all out and left them in the sink. "Sorry about that."

"I don't think anything you did caused that," I replied, the bitter taste lingering in my mouth.

He smiled slightly as he stared out the kitchen window. After a few minutes, he took a deep breath, exhaled sharply, and turned to look at me. "I guess it's time to go home then."

"I guess so. Is there anything else I can do for you? Anything you need?"

"I don't know. I don't think so. Not now."

"Okay then," I said, getting up. I walked over to him and gave him a quick hug. "If you think of anything, let me know. You know where to find me."

"Thanks," he said.

"Seriously, Matty, I know I didn't want to ask anybody for anything those first few days, but I needed the help. There's a lot to take care of. Just ask."

He smiled sadly. "You know, you're the only person who still calls me Matty."

"You're the only person who still calls me Franny."

"What do people call you now, Franny?" he asked.

"Fran, Francesca." I shrugged. "Mostly Francesca in New York, mostly Fran here. Just depends on who's doing the calling."

"I see," he said.

"Everyone calls you Matt now, huh?"

"Yup... but you can still call me Matty if you want."

I smiled. "We'll see. We're not five years old anymore. But you're welcome to keep calling me Franny."

"Will do, *Franny*," he replied.

I chuckled softly. "I guess I'd better get going then."

"All right. I'll see you."

"See you."

Matty walked me to the door. I headed off to my house and my bed, which I knew I wouldn't be able to fall asleep in because of thoughts of my mother and Mr. Cardosi.

Chapter Five

I tried to help Matty as much as I could over the next few days. He took some time off work to deal with his dad's estate and funeral arrangements, and I cut back on my hours at the café. I still went in every day, just not for the full fourteen hours it was open. Since I'd just been through everything Matty was dealing with, I was able to suggest some things (go ahead and file for the life insurance so you can use the money for the funeral), warn him about others (the funeral home will charge you for those "refreshments" they so casually offer), and help him with the rest (how about the café provides the refreshments– my coffee will be better than the funeral home's any day).

It helped that Matty and I had been friends for most of our lives. I was able to pick out meaningful pictures of Mr. Cardosi to display at the funeral home, particularly ones with Matty and the late Mrs. Cardosi or ones from special times they'd shared. I helped Matty go through some of his dad's things, even pulling out some mementos of Matty's mom that he'd never known existed.

As much as I wanted to help my friend in his time of need, part of the reason I felt so strongly that I needed to help Matty was because I'd been the one who found his dad's body. Sure, he had repeatedly expressed his gratitude to me for finding his dad and all, but that didn't make me feel much better about it. I felt somehow responsible for what had happened, so I wanted to do as much as I could to help out. I wouldn't say that I didn't enjoy spending so much time with Matty again though.

It took several days for the autopsy to be completed, and we obviously couldn't have the funeral until after it was done, so

Mr. Cardosi wasn't buried until a week and a half after he'd died. I was glad for Matty when the medical examiner's office finally released the body. I knew it was wearing on Matty for things to take that long. I saw it in his eyes and the way he carried himself. He didn't magically stop being sad after the funeral, but at least he was finally able to get back to his normal routine and not spend all day, every day, thinking about his dad's death.

After we both went back to our jobs, we didn't see each other as much. In fact, I'd only seen him once since the funeral, when he showed up in the café one day shortly after the lunch rush ended. We didn't offer a lot of food, just some pastries and sandwiches, but that didn't stop the tourists from flocking in to get something to take back to the beach.

Sammy, Becky, and I were all working. Becky was in the back washing coffee cups, Sammy was wiping down the counters, and I was making some fresh mozzarella-tomato-basil sandwiches to go in the refrigerator case. I heard the door jingle open but didn't look up from what I was doing, since Sammy was closer to the register.

Until I heard her whisper, "It's Matt!"

I looked over my shoulder. Sure enough, it was Matty. I was surprised to see him because, even though he lived in Cape Bay, he actually worked a couple of towns over. If we saw him at the café, it was usually first thing in the morning or just before close. I was surprised by how happy I was to see him. I'd enjoyed spending time with him, but I didn't realize how much I'd missed him until he walked in.

"Hello!" Sammy said in a singsong tone. "What can I get for you today?"

"I got it," I said, wiping my hands on my apron. "Can you finish up the sandwiches?"

"Sure thing," she replied, moving over to my station. "Nice to see you, Matt!"

Sammy's cheerfulness and friendliness were part of what made her such a great employee. We had customers who I swore came in just because they liked to talk to her. We also had customers who I thought came in just because Sammy wasn't bad to look at. She had a round cherub face to go with her blond angel hair and soft curves that I'd heard made men think about cuddling up with her on cold winter nights. But she, of course, had been seeing the same guy for almost ten years. He lived with his mother and said he couldn't possibly get married and leave her because it would break her heart. Why he wasn't as concerned about Sammy's heart, I didn't know. In any case, the men who came in to flirt with her didn't seem to bother Sammy.

I smiled at Matty. "Caffè mocha?" I confirmed, already starting the drink.

"Yeah," he answered simply.

I looked at him as I pulled the espresso. Something didn't seem right, and it wasn't that he was reaching for his wallet. "Put that away, Matty. It's on me."

He didn't argue, just shrugged and shoved his wallet back in his pocket. Something was definitely bothering him.

"Go ahead, sit down," I said. "I'll bring it over in just a minute."

Matty nodded and walked over to sit at a corner table. I made a second drink, that one for myself, while I worked on creating a sunrise in the foam of Matty's drink. It had been one of my favorite patterns in the weeks after my mother passed away. It reminded me that no matter how bad any given day was, there was always another day coming, and life went on. I finished it just in time to pour the milk on my own drink. Since it was just for me, I wasn't going to bother creating something terribly intricate, but sometimes I seemed physically incapable of not putting some kind of design in a latte. I poured in a quick rosetta.

I pulled off my apron and picked up the two cups and saucers to take over to Matty's table. "I'm going to take a quick break," I told Sammy as I walked past her.

"Sounds good!" she chirped.

I heard the smile in her voice. Since Mr. Cardosi's funeral, I'd actually cut back on my hours, and Sammy was happy about it. She'd been genuinely concerned about me working so much—that cheerfulness and friendliness wasn't just an act. As much as I hated to admit it, I was happier too now that I was working closer to forty hours each week instead of one hundred.

I set the cups on Matty's table, careful to make sure his was positioned properly. "Mind if I join you?"

"No, actually, that's why I'm here," he replied.

"We haven't seen each other much since the funeral."

"Yeah, I know, I've been catching up at work. They didn't mind me being gone for two weeks, but that doesn't mean the paperwork didn't pile up my desk." Matty worked as a project manager at a telecom engineering company. He'd told me the engineers who worked under him could manage pretty well without him, but he still had to sign off on everything they did. If something on the project went wrong, he was the one who would get fired, not them.

"I can imagine." I knew how bad it used to get when I'd take just a couple of days off at my job in New York. I couldn't imagine how long it would take to get caught up after being out for two whole weeks.

Matty looked at the design in his coffee. "Sunrise?"

"Yup," I responded. "New beginnings, new life. It's always darkest before the sunrise—"

"It's always darkest before the dawn," Matty corrected.

"Same thing." I took a sip of my coffee. It was much better than that bitter brew we'd had the night Mr. Cardosi had died. Not that I was patting myself on the back—just about anything would have been better than that foul concoction.

"I almost hate to drink it," Matty said. "I don't want to mess it up."

"But the coffee's the best part!" I retorted. "It's the whole point! The cappuccino art is just there to enhance the experience. We eat—and drink—with our eyes first, you know."

My grandfather's motto had been: "Make your food delicious, and make it beautiful." He would never tolerate me serving a sloppy mess of food or drink to a customer, and he'd insisted I make it again and again until I got it right.

"You're the designer," Matty said as he raised the cup to his lips. His eyes rolled back a little as he tasted it. "God, this is amazing! You seriously make the best coffee I've ever tasted. I don't know how you do it."

"Amaro family secret." I smiled, taking another sip. We really did make some amazing coffee. Well, I guess I made amazing coffee, since I was the only Amaro left. "Here, have a cupcake."

I gave him one of the chocolate cupcakes from behind the counter. We didn't exclusively sell Italian drinks and desserts. After all, customers were crazy about cupcakes, and I made sure we stocked at least four flavors a day.

"This is heaven," Matty said. "I always get the chocolate when I come here. How did you know?"

"You can't go wrong with chocolate." I had one myself. They were dark chocolate, with the most delicious peanut butter filling that our bakers made to perfection.

We enjoyed our coffee and cupcakes for a few more minutes before Matty pulled out a file folder. He drummed his fingers on it. "I guess I should tell you why I'm here."

"I thought it was for the pleasant company and the delicious coffee," I joked.

"I wish that's what it was. Mike called me this morning and asked me to come down to the police station. The medical examiner finished up the report on my dad's autopsy, and Mike wanted to give me the results." He was silent for what seemed like a very long time.

"And?" I asked, deciding that it was up to me to break the silence.

Matty pushed the folder toward me.

"What's this?" I asked.

"That's the autopsy report."

"You want me to read it?" I whispered.

He opened his mouth then closed it again and just nodded. From the look on his face, I wasn't sure he could have spoken if he'd wanted to.

My stomach clenched as I opened the folder. A picture of Mr. Cardosi was on the top, stapled to a report bearing the words "Autopsy Report: Office of the Medical Examiner of the Commonwealth of Massachusetts" across the top. I looked at Matty. His face was drawn. I resisted the urge to reach across the table and take the hand he rested there.

I looked back down and read the report. There was a lot of medical jargon and terminology I didn't really understand. It went through the physical examination and findings in detail, including specific information about Mr. Cardosi's health prior to his passing. I kept reading, absorbing what I could. No tumors, no significant narrowing of the arteries, no brain abnormalities, no blood clots, some mild arthritis. It appeared that for an older man, Mr. Cardosi had been in excellent health. Then I saw what must have caused that look on Matty's face.

Significant presence of potassium cyanide in blood, tissues, and digestive system...

consistent with intentional poisoning... until further investigation can be completed, the medical examiner's office determines the cause of death to be homicide.

"Dear God," I whispered. I looked at it again, certain I had misunderstood, but I hadn't. It almost looked as if the words "cyanide," "poison," and "homicide" were in bigger, bolder print than the surrounding text, but when I looked closely, I could tell they weren't—it was just the horror of them that made them seem that way. "Poison?" I looked at Matty. "Poison?" I said louder, as the weight of it came down on me.

I must have said it louder than I thought because I heard a clatter from the backroom and saw the few lingering afternoon customers look at me.

I gave them all a smile and a little wave. "Sorry!" I hoped they would all just think I was talking about Poison the band, not poison the killer. "Matty, what—? Who—?" I couldn't get words out of my mouth. I had so many questions. I couldn't comprehend what I was reading.

"I don't know," Matty said. "They don't know. Mike said they'll do an investigation, but—"

"But what?" I asked.

"But with the amount of cyanide in his system, death would have been nearly instantaneous."

I looked at Matty, trying to process what he was saying. "Do they think someone injected him? Like some lunatic ran up while he was sitting on the back patio and stabbed him with it?"

Matty shook his head. "He ingested it."

"What? Like a cyanide capsule? Like spies use to kill themselves if they're captured by the enemy?"

"No. More like a food... or a drink."

Then it dawned on me. *Ingested. Nearly instantaneous.* "The coffee!" I gasped.

Matty nodded, covering his face with his hands. I couldn't believe it. Someone had snuck cyanide into Mr. Cardosi's coffee to murder him. Then another thought occurred to me.

"The autopsy report said homicide."

Matty nodded.

"But they don't think he could have—" I wasn't sure how to even say the rest. "Done it to himself?"

Matty dragged his hands down his face. After a minute, he said, "No. I asked Mike the same thing. He said that since there was no note and no indication that he might have been considering it, and he still had most of a pot of coffee inside, they're going to investigate it as a murder. I mean, why would you make a whole pot of coffee if you just needed one cup to kill yourself, right?"

I nodded. It didn't make sense. Not unless you added the poison to the pot itself, thinking you might need more than one cup, but even then, why not just add more poison to the one cup? Then I had another terrible thought. "Matty?"

"Yeah, Franny?"

"What if the whole coffeepot was poisoned? We drank out of that coffee pot."

Matty held up a hand and shook his head. "I thought of that. Mike said pouring it out and rinsing it before we made another pot would probably have gotten rid of all the poison. And that we'd be long since dead if it didn't."

That was a relief. Although I felt bad being relieved about anything at a time like this.

Matty continued. "I'm going to meet Mike over at Dad's house later this afternoon so he can take the coffeepot into evidence. He said there's a good chance they won't find anything, especially because we used it afterward, but they'll give it a shot."

I took another sip of my coffee. "You don't think that's why the coffee tasted so bad, do you? Did Mike say what cyanide tastes like?"

"Bitter almonds, apparently. But I've had coffee at my dad's before. It was always pretty bad. I don't know if it was the coffeemaker or the kind he bought, but I don't think there was any way to redeem that stuff."

I nodded thoughtfully. The best technique can't save a bad brewer and bad beans. I glanced at the autopsy report again. It was so hard to believe. Even when Mike had been asking us a million questions and taking pictures of the house, I didn't ever really think something criminal had taken place. A heart attack or stroke just seemed like the most obvious culprits. And it had turned out to be a human culprit instead.

Matty looked at the wrought-iron clock on the wall. "I better get going if I'm going to be on time to meet Mike." He drained his coffee cup and set it back on the saucer. "Thanks for the coffee. Are you sure I can't pay you for it?"

"Absolutely not." I closed the folder and slid it back across the table to Matty. "Thank you for letting me know about the autopsy."

"I needed to talk to someone about it, and I knew you wouldn't say anything incredibly insensitive." He shook his head. "You wouldn't believe some of the stuff I've heard."

"Oh, I think I would. People have said some pretty awful stuff to me too. It's like they don't even think about what it sounds like to the person they're talking to."

Matty picked up the folder and tapped it on the table. "Well, I'm sure once word about this gets out, there'll be a whole new round of gossip."

"I'm sure there will." Cape Bay was a small town and news, especially sordid news, traveled fast in any small town.

Matty stood to leave. "Thanks again for the coffee."

"No problem," I replied, standing also. I picked up our empty cups to take into the back to be washed. "Let me know if you hear anything else."

"Will do. See you later."

I gestured good-bye with one of the cups as he left, then I went back to work behind the counter.

Chapter Six

I worked until close that night. I'd found that I preferred to come in around lunchtime and work through the afternoon. I'd always been a bit of a night owl, so even if I got off work in the early afternoon, I'd end up staying up way too late. Then I'd be dragging when I opened the café at six. Sammy was a morning person, though, so it worked out for her to handle the morning shift.

Right after Matty left, we got busy again as all the tourists came in off the beach and wanted to get something to eat or drink. One of the restaurants down the street had live music every night, so the evening crowd always had an atmosphere of gearing up for a party.

The customers kept my mind off Matty and the medical examiner's findings while I was at work, but once I got home and curled up on the couch with a book and a glass of red wine, my mind wandered back to our conversation. I was still in shock over what the autopsy report had said. The idea that someone had come into Mr. Cardosi's house and put cyanide in his coffee was just unfathomable. Who was it? Why would they do such a thing? It must have been someone Mr. Cardosi knew if he let them get that close to him. But Matty had said that his dad didn't have any real friends. On the other hand, Mrs. Collins had been pretty eager to get into the house. Maybe she wanted to see if she'd left any evidence behind? Maybe to dump and wash the contaminated coffee pot? It was a viable theory.

I stopped myself. It was not a viable theory. It was ridiculous. And besides, what business was it of mine? I was a former public relations manager turned café owner and artisan barista, not a detective. Sure, I'd read a mystery novel or two (or twenty), but it wasn't as though I was a professional or someone with any kind of background that would allow me to speculate on someone's motives. Besides, the police were investigating. I went back to reading my book.

On my second glass of wine, I started thinking that since I'd been the first one at the scene—I was thinking of it as "the scene" now—maybe I did have some qualification to do a little investigating. After all, I'd been the only one to see it as it originally was. I may have noticed something that no one else did. And the police didn't know about Mrs. Collins. They hadn't been there when the crowd spoke to Matty and me. Maybe I should just tell the police about it. But what if Mrs. Collins really was just a friend of Mr. Cardosi and had been making a genuine offer to help us? Or even just a meddling old woman? She didn't deserve to be investigated by the police for that. Maybe tomorrow before work I could just go over and have a neighborly little chat with her. I wondered if she was still awake.

I got up off the couch and crept across the living room to peep out the blinds. Mrs. Collins's house was dark. Of course it was. It was after ten, and all the old folks on our street went to bed by nine. I went back to the couch and curled back up with my book and my wine. I tried to think over what else I had seen that day that Mike might not have noticed. I remembered that the front door had been unlocked when Matty and I went in. I was supposed to tell Mike about it, but it had completely slipped my mind, and Matty's too, I guessed. That was another clue.

A *clue*. I scoffed at myself. Now I really was being ridiculous, thinking about clues and suspects. Even so, I got up and found a notepad by the phone to make some notes on. Notes of things I had to remember to mention to the police, I told myself, not notes about what investigating I was going to do. Although it wouldn't hurt to at least check a few things before I went to the police with them. I didn't want to bother Mike with a bunch of details that seemed relevant to me when he probably had much more important leads to chase.

I wrote down odd things I remembered— Mrs. Collins, the door—then I thought that it might be good for me to write down everything exactly as I remembered it before my memory faded. It had already been weeks since the murder, and even though I thought I remembered everything clearly, I'd probably forgotten more details than I realized. I thought I remembered something about that from my college psychology class—something about how memories fade and get altered. That was why I needed to write everything down *now*.

I flipped to a fresh page and wrote down absolutely everything I could remember about that day, starting from my walk home. I read something once about how you can remember more if you tie it to sense memories, so I wrote down the color of the sky, the temperature, how windy it was, what the grass had smelled like—every sight, sound, or smell I could remember. Then I thought about how Mike had asked about the last time I saw Mr. Cardosi, so I flipped to another page and wrote down everything I remembered about every encounter I'd had with him since I got back to town.

By the time I was finished, it was well after midnight and I was itching to talk to Matty to see if he remembered something that I'd forgotten. I could ask him more about some of what he'd said to Mike, specifically what he'd said about Mr. Cardosi's enemies being more in his head than in real life. Apparently at least one of those enemies was in real life. It was way too late to call, so I pulled out my cell phone and sent Matty a text asking if he wanted to meet for breakfast. Getting up that early would be rough, but I wanted to talk to Matty as soon as possible.

I went upstairs to my old childhood bedroom and got ready to go to sleep. I plugged my phone into the wall next to the bed and made sure the volume was turned all the way up. I wanted to make sure I heard it if Matty texted me back, so I put the phone right next to my head. I thought it would be impossible to fall asleep with all of the thoughts whirling through my head, but it seemed like only a few seconds later, Matty was texting me at six in the morning.

I jumped out of bed with more energy than I remembered having in the morning since high school and got dressed as quickly as I could. I took the long way to the café, out along the street instead of cutting through the neighbors' backyards. I hadn't taken the shortcut since the day Mr. Cardosi died, and I wasn't sure I'd be up to it again for a long time. Part of me thought I should always take it in case someone else was dead in their backyard, waiting to be discovered by a passerby, but the more logical part of me prevailed. Either that or I gave in to the fear that I actually would find another body. I guess it just depended on how I looked at it.

I got to the café before Matty, so I hurried in behind the counter to fix our drinks. Matty always—always, like, since high school—got a caffè mocha, so I didn't have to wait for him to arrive to find out what he wanted.

"Uh, Francesca?" Sammy asked as I grabbed cups and saucers.

"Yeah?"

"You know it's six thirty in the morning, right?"

"Oh, yeah, I know," I said.

"Are you feeling okay?"

"Yeah, why?"

Sammy just looked at me for a second. "Because it's six thirty in the morning and you're *here* and you're *perky*."

"Oh, I'm just meeting Matty for breakfast."

"Matt Cardosi?" Sammy asked.

"Yep." I had my milk steaming and was ready to pull the espresso.

"Didn't you have coffee with him yesterday afternoon? Francesca Amaro, do you have something to tell me?"

I wrinkled my forehead. What? How did she know about Matty's dad? Was it all over town already? Had we been talking that loudly yesterday? Then I noticed the look on her face and realized that wasn't what she'd meant at all. "Oh no, nothing like that. It's—it's actually something about his dad."

Before I could say anything else, Sammy leaned toward me. "Oh my gosh, have you heard? Karen Maynard, who works over at the police department, was in here when I opened up because she likes to get a cup of coffee before she goes and works out. She told me they think Mr. Cardosi was murdered!"

I was surprised. I had never known Sammy to be much of a gossip, but then again, we didn't really get much murder-level gossip in Cape Bay. The grapevine usually only discussed who took whose seat at a luncheon or who skipped the knitting club the night they were making sweaters for teddy bears to give to Sherpa children in Nepal.

"Oh, of course you know. You're good friends with Matt." Sammy stopped for a second. "He *did* tell you, right? I'm not breaking this news to you now, am I?"

"No, you're not," I said, perhaps a little curtly.

The bell on the door jingled before Sammy could say anything else. It was Matty.

"Good morning!" I called. "What do you want for breakfast? We have fruit bowls, parfaits, muffins, cupcakes... come look in the case and see what looks good." I poured the milk in Matty's coffee as I talked. I had decided on a butterfly to continue the theme of rebirth and renewal.

"You're going to let me pay today, right?" Matty said as he walked over. He looked handsome, dressed for work in gray pants and a crisp white dress shirt.

"Nope," I answered. "I asked you to meet me, so it's on me."

"You don't have to do that, Franny."

"Of course I do." I put his finished coffee aside and started working on mine.

"How are the snickerdoodle cupcakes?" Matty asked, inspecting the contents of the display case.

"You want a cupcake for breakfast?" I asked.

"Hey, you offered!"

"They're amazing!" Sammy interjected. "The cinnamon buttercream icing is to die for. Francesca made the cupcakes last night before she left, and you know how good her baking is."

"That I do," Matty replied as Sammy handed a wax paper-wrapped cupcake across the counter.

"Drinks are almost ready," I told him. "Make yourself comfortable, and I'll be right over."

Today, Matty chose a comfortable armchair in what my mother had called the "Chatty Cathy Corner." It was the corner with the most comfortable chairs where, during the school year, the stay-at-home moms would settle in for the better part of the school day. When I was growing up, Cathy Sampson had been one of the most dedicated sit-and-talkers, and so that section of the café was named. It didn't help that Cathy had been known to make snide comments about my mother being a single parent when she wasn't quite out of earshot. My mother would just smile sweetly through clenched teeth then go in the backroom and mutter to my grandmother about it.

I finished off my coffee, pouring a leaf into the foam. Another simple design but still beautiful. I carried our two cups of coffee over to the table between the chairs Matty had selected. His cupcake was sitting on the table, still wrapped up. I guessed he was waiting for me to get there with the coffee.

"What are you going to eat?" Matty asked.

"Oh, I completely forgot!" That happened sometimes when I was focused on coffee. I went back and grabbed a parfait out of the case and a spoon from the container on the counter. I made my way back over to the Chatty Cathy Corner and sat in one of the armchairs.

Matty unwrapped his cupcake and took a bite. "Oh, it's delicious, Franny!"

"Thank you." I smiled, taking a spoonful of my parfait. "How's the coffee?"

Matty looked at it. "I like the butterfly." He took a sip. "Excellent."

"Good. Sometimes I'm not so sure this early in the morning."

"I don't think you've made a bad cup of coffee in your life."

I thought for a moment. "No, I did once when I was nine."

Matty laughed and almost spit his coffee at me. "I'm not even sure that's true," he said when he'd recovered. We each ate a little bit more of our breakfast, then Matty leaned back in his chair. "So what's up? What did you want to talk about so badly that you texted me at one in the morning?"

I took a deep breath. "I was doing some thinking last night. About your dad. And how he died."

Matty nodded, looking as though he wasn't quite sure what to expect me to say next.

"And I want to ask you a few questions."

Chapter Seven

"You want to ask me a few questions," Matty repeated. "About my dad?"

I swallowed hard. "Yeah, I mean, I was thinking last night—"

The look on Matty's face stopped me mid-sentence. His eyebrows were raised, and he was looking at me as if antlers were growing out of my head.

After several seconds of silence, Matty spoke. "You were thinking?"

"Um, yeah. It's just..." I took a deep breath. "Last night, I remembered that we never told Mike that the door was unlocked. And then there was the thing with Mrs. Collins..." I hesitated again.

Matty wasn't quite looking at me as though I was crazy anymore. That was a good thing.

"And I realized there might be more that we forgot to tell him. Or that we didn't realize at the time might be important, and now that we know he was—how he died—they might be important. And I just thought it might be good for us to go over things."

Matty just looked at me.

"You know, if you want to." I tried to read his expression, but I couldn't. I didn't know if he would be mad at me for wanting to investigate his dad's murder or interested in working with me. I suddenly felt that this may have been a very bad idea.

After what seemed like an eternity, Matty shrugged. "Can't hurt."

Relief flooded me, and I smiled. "Great!"

"So what did you want to know?"

"Well, I've already written down everything I remember from that day. I know Mike asked you this that day, but what I really want to know is, now that we know your dad was—I mean, how he died—I was wondering if you can think of anyone who might have wanted to hurt your dad."

Matty sighed and adjusted his position in his chair. "You're looking for suspects, huh?"

"Uh, I, uh, um—"

A half smile crept across Matty's face. "You can say yes. I'm not the police. I don't care who finds out who murdered my dad, as long as someone does and the guy—or girl, I guess—goes to jail. If you asking some questions gets things done faster, ask away."

I exhaled the breath I hadn't realized I was holding and smiled. "So can you think of anyone?"

Matty tipped his head toward the ceiling in thought. He let out a long breath. "Well, you know how Dad was."

I noticed that he'd gotten used to using the past tense in reference to his dad. It was an inevitable part of the grieving process, an important part actually, but in a way, it was still sad, as if he was finally giving up his dad.

"He thought everybody was out to get him." Matty laughed softly. "I guess there actually was at least one person who was." He shook his head. "Anyway, the conspiracies against him were *mostly* all in his head, but that didn't mean he didn't make enemies. It was almost a talent of his. I've never met anybody who could hold a grudge like him—and against so many people too. You know how there's that new haircut place down the street?" He pointed down Main Street toward the beach.

I nodded. It wasn't really new, but it was new to us. It had probably been there about ten years or so.

"Half the men in town go there now. Not because they prefer it to my dad's place but because he banned them. If somebody said they didn't like their haircut, banned. If they complained about having to wait, banned. If they didn't tip enough, banned. Half the time, they didn't even know until they showed up for their next haircut and he started waving his comb at them, telling them to get out and they weren't welcome. I think some of the guys don't even know *why* they were banned." He chuckled. "You know, I think one time he actually kicked out the wrong guy. It was the guy's brother or something. He kicked him out then realized later it was the wrong guy, but he'd never admit he was wrong about something like that, so both brothers were banned."

"That's pretty hardcore," I said.

"Yeah, Dad didn't back down." His face lit up, and he leaned across the table toward me. His eyes were sparkling. "One time, and I shouldn't laugh about this, but"–he laughed–"right in the middle of his haircut, some guy said something bad about the Sox–this was back before they'd won the World Series–he said something about they sucked and they'd never win and the Yankees were so much better. Dad just took his clippers and shaved right down the middle of the guy's head. I guess he wasn't looking in the mirror, so Dad kept going and shaved the guy's whole damn head before he realized what was going on. Oh my God, the guy stormed out, swearing at my dad. When Dad came home and told me about it, he didn't even care that the guy didn't pay–he was just so happy about shaving his head."

I giggled as I pictured the scene. My grandparents had emphasized customer service, so I couldn't imagine treating a customer like that, but it was funny to think about. I was enjoying the story so much I almost forgot that I was supposed to be looking for suspects. "Was there anybody your dad had been feuding with recently?"

Matty leaned back again and crossed his arms thoughtfully. I took a drink of my coffee while I waited.

Finally he sighed. "He'd been complaining a lot about the cell phone store across the street from the shop. He thought the signs in the windows were tacky and the guy who runs it was a jerk. He really hated when they had somebody out front dancing around in one of those giant squishy cell phone costumes." Matty chuckled. "That drove him nuts. I remember him yelling that you didn't see him having someone dress up as a giant pair of scissors and dance around outside the barbershop. 'If you need someone to dance around dressed up like what you sell, you must not be a very good salesman!'"

"Do you know if they ever spoke? Or did your dad just complain about him?" I asked.

"Oh, they had words," Matty replied. "You think my dad would pass up that opportunity? I know Dad went in there at least once because he was telling me about the cheesy cell phone cases the guy was selling. It annoyed the hell out of Dad for some reason. I mean, he didn't need to go in there and look at them. He didn't even have a cell phone that one of those cases would fit. I guess the guy just got under his skin for some reason. Dad yelled at him plenty from across the street, and the guy yelled back. I've seen him out there a couple times. He doesn't seem like the nicest guy anyway. Kind of a jerk. Really arrogant. I'm not surprised Dad couldn't stand him."

"Was it personal?"

Matty scoffed. "Everything was personal with Dad."

"Do you think it was personal for the other guy?"

He shrugged. "Hard to know. I mean, like I said, he seems like a jerk, but I kind of think he was just playing with Dad, antagonizing him because it was fun for him to see Dad get so angry. I don't know if he actually disliked Dad though. Especially enough to kill him." He stopped and drummed his fingers on the table. "Of course, until we got that autopsy report, I didn't think anyone disliked Dad enough to kill him." He took a deep breath. "But can you imagine being mad enough about getting blacklisted from a barbershop to kill somebody? What else could it have been? It's not like it was random."

"Well, I guess Cell Phone Guy is a place to start," I said. "Your dad didn't keep a list of who he banned, did he?"

Matty laughed. "With my dad's memory for imaginary offenses, he didn't need to keep a list. I swear he could remember–in detail!–people who pissed him off before I was born. He once told me a story about a guy who cut him off in traffic in 1976!"

"So I'll start with Cell Phone Guy and work my way back. Did he happen to give you the name and contact information of the guy from 1976?"

Matty grinned. "No, but if that guy came back to kill him after all these years, he even beats my dad at holding a grudge!"

I laughed with Matty. I certainly hoped for the sake of everyone involved that neither the police nor I had to go that far back through Mr. Cardosi's history to find out who killed him.

"So you have any more questions?" Matty asked after we stopped laughing.

I thought back over my notes from the night before. For some reason, I hadn't thought to bring my notepad with me. I'd either have to go home to get it before I went to talk to Cell Phone Guy or run by the drugstore and pick up a new one. A new one would probably be good. The one at home was a giant yellow legal pad—not very subtle for toting around town.

"I don't think so," I said, unable to think of anything else I needed to ask him.

He glanced at the clock on the wall and groaned. "Looks like I have to get going anyway. Thank you for breakfast."

"No problem at all," I replied. "Someone's got to eat all this stuff."

"Oh, I don't think you'll have a problem with that," Matty said, patting his stomach. "You know your baking is out of this world."

I waved dismissively even though I knew my baking really was good. A little humility never hurt anyone. Matty stood to leave, and I was surprisingly sad that he had to go. I knew we couldn't linger here all day, but I enjoyed talking to him and wasn't quite ready for it to end. I stood and gave him a hug. A piece of his hair fell down over his forehead, and I reflexively pushed it back before realizing that that was something of an intimate gesture. Matty didn't seem to notice or mind though.

"Guess I need to see about getting that cut, huh?" he said, sounding a little sad.

"I'll probably be joining everyone from my dad's blacklist down the street."

"The barbershop's still open though, isn't it?" I asked. Mr. Cardosi had two part-time barbers who worked with him, old-timers like him, and they'd been working since his death. As far as I knew, Matty didn't have any plans to close the shop, at least not until his dad's estate was fully settled and he knew what he was dealing with.

"Yeah, but Dad's the only one who ever cut my hair, and I don't think I could stand going in there and having someone else do it. It'll be weird enough going to a stranger, but I think it'll be easier."

I nodded sympathetically. I knew from experience that every day brought new reminders of a parent's passing, and in the most unexpected of places.

"Anyway," Matty said, shaking his head and shaking that piece of hair back onto his forehead. This time he shoved it back. "Anyway, I've got to get going if I'm going to make it to work on time."

We said good-bye, and he left, waving at me before he let the door close behind him. I gathered up our dishes and took them to the backroom to be washed.

"You guys have a nice chat?" Sammy asked.

"Yup," I said, not really feeling the need to elaborate.

"He doing okay?"

I looked at her. She looked as though she was back to regular good-hearted, compassionate Sammy instead of the gossipy Sammy from earlier.

"Yeah, he's doing okay," I said.

"Are *you* okay?" she asked.

I was a little surprised, and it must have shown on my face.

"It's just—with you losing your mom so recently and all, and then finding Mr. Cardosi's body, and you being so close to Matt—" She shrugged. "I just wanted to make sure you're doing okay. I don't ask enough. Some days coffee is all we talk about."

I stared at her for a minute then pulled her into a hug. I was actually moved by her concern for me. "Thank you."

Sammy rubbed my back vigorously. "That's what friends are for."

Friends. Somehow I hadn't actually thought of Sammy as my friend until that moment. She was my mom's friend if anything, but mostly just a coworker. But Sammy really had been there for me as a friend since I'd been back in town. Everything she'd done to help me get back into the swing of things at the café and to get everything for my mother in order had been the actions of a friend, not just a coworker or an employee. I hugged her a little tighter before we let go.

"Well, thank you for being my friend," I said.

Her big blue eyes smiled back at me. "I'm happy to do it. So are you going back home or are you sticking around for a while? I'm sure you can find something to do around here, but Becky and I have everything nailed down on our own if you want to go home and get a nap or something. I know this is still early for you." She grinned. My night-owl habits were no secret to her.

I looked around the café, which was still mostly empty. I knew the drugstore wouldn't open for at least a half hour yet and the cell phone shop would be closed for an hour or two after that, so I had some time to kill. It didn't look as though my coffee-making skills would be in much demand for the next little while. I had plenty to think about after my late night and my talk with Matty, though, so it might be good for me to get out of my home-and-café rut and go do something else for a little while.

"You know what?" I said to Sammy with a gleam in my eye. "I think I might go for a little walk on the beach."

Sammy smiled. I knew she was happy to hear that I was doing something for myself for a change. "I think that's an excellent idea."

Chapter Eight

The morning was still cool as I stepped out of the café and headed toward the beach. I breathed the salt air deep into my lungs. Even though I'd grown up there and preferred to take my vacations in the mountains, far away from the seaside, I understood why people came. There was something restorative about the sea breezes. Standing at the edge of the world, the water swirling around your feet and inching you deeper into the sand, while staring off at the expanse of the ocean is grounding. Some people said it made them feel small, but it didn't do that for me. It made me feel a part of something big.

I pulled the legs of my jeans up toward my knee. One advantage of the skin-tight cigarette-style jeans that were in style was that they had a lot of stretch. I kicked off my shoes and carried them as I crossed the dune and stepped onto the sand. I smiled at the feeling of fine grains between my toes. I couldn't believe I'd been home for so long and hadn't come down to the beach.

I walked to the water's edge and let the waves wash over my feet. They were cold, but I held my ground. The water was always cold there—not like some of the beaches farther south that my college friends had visited for spring break. Those had always felt like bathwater to me.

I pulled my feet out of the sand and walked a little farther so that the water came up around my calves when the waves came in. I was one of the few people out there at that in-between hour. The people who came out to watch the sunrise had gone home, and the families wanting to play on the beach wouldn't be out for a while yet. It was just me, some seashell searchers, and a few fishermen reclining on chairs, their lines cast deep into the water. It was the most peaceful I'd felt in a long time.

I stood in the water for a while until the incoming tide threatened to soak my pants. I walked back a few yards and sat in the sand. I could always brush off my pants later or, if that proved too difficult, walk home and change. I watched the ocean change colors as the sun inched up in the sky. When the first tourists appeared on the beach, the family patriarchs weighed down with beach chairs and coolers and umbrellas and sand toys and more beach paraphernalia that I didn't know how they managed to carry, I decided it was time to head back to town and my investigation.

I made my way up off the beach and rinsed my feet at the spigot on the other side of the dune. When I felt as though I was sufficiently de-beached, I pulled the legs of my jeans back down and slid my shoes back on my feet. I walked up to the drugstore to get a less obtrusive notebook. I found a little spiral-bound one like Mike's. I figured if it was small and portable enough for him, it was small and portable enough for me. I picked up a two-pack of pens too. Purchases in hand, I headed back out on the street. I checked the time. The cell phone shop was probably open, so I walked up in that direction. When I came to the block where the barbershop and the cell phone store were, I stopped and stood at the corner for a few minutes.

Matty and Mr. Cardosi were right—the signs on the front of the store were incredibly tacky. They were bright yellow and red, with giant print and lots of exclamation points. "Cell Phone Accessories!!!" they screamed. "Lowest prices in town!!!!!" "Styles You Can't Find Anywhere Else!!!!" It was pretty obnoxious.

I decided to pretend I was in the market for a new cell phone case. I figured it was better not to start asking questions right away. Let him think I was just some random person coming in to look around and chit-chat a bit.

I walked down the street slowly, looking in all the shops as though I was just out doing some window shopping. I got up to the barbershop then looked across the street at the cell phone store. I made a beeline across the street, thinking that if anyone saw me, they'd assume I just really wanted a new cell phone case. I pushed open the door to the sound of a loud, annoying electronic jangle. Rock music played over the speaker system. Not exactly what I thought of when I thought about customer-friendly music, but if it worked for them, who was I to judge?

"I'll be out in a sec!" a voice called from the back.

I looked around at the displays. I had to hand it to Mr. Cardosi—he hadn't been wrong. A lot of the cases were pretty tacky. They looked like something only a teenager would buy. And a teenager with poor taste at that.

"What's up?" the owner of the voice said as he emerged from the back.

What's up? Who greets a customer with "What's up?" But instead of asking him what was wrong with him, I turned toward him with a smile. "Hi!"

When he actually looked at me, he grinned. "Well, hello there! Haven't seen you around here before!"

I shrugged. "Kinda new in town." That wasn't really a lie. I had only come back recently.

"Oh well, let me be the first to welcome you," he said, strolling up to me.

"I'm not *that* new." If he thought I'd just gotten there that week, my plan wouldn't work.

"One of the first then." He smirked.

I put on the most genuine smile I could. "Well, thank you."

He stepped around me and leaned against the display so he was looking at me straight on. He gave off a major sleazy salesman vibe while at the same time being completely unprofessional. His blond hair was slicked back with way more gel than was necessary, and he had a permanent smirk. His teeth were way too white in his darkly tanned face, and his clothes screamed former prep school boy.

"So where'd you move here from..." He implicitly invited me to give him my name.

"Francesca. And New York. I moved here from New York." I extended my hand to shake.

"Well, hello, *Francesca*," he said, taking my hand. His hand was clammy, and he held on much longer than he needed to.

After what I felt was a sufficiently polite amount of time, I withdrew my hand and tried to subtly wipe his sweat off on my jeans.

"I'm Chris. Chris Tompson. New York, eh?" he went on. "What brought you to sleepy Cape Bay from the big city?"

I tried to think fast. If I didn't tell him I ran Antonia's and he found out later, he'd know I'd been playing him. But if I told him, he might figure out that I wasn't all that new in town. Best to just sidestep the issue and hope it didn't come back to bite me. Once I got the information I needed, it wouldn't much matter if he knew I'd stretched the truth.

"Slower pace of life." I smiled. "You know, New York is so busy and hectic. I just wanted to be able to kick back and relax a little. Not stress so much. You hear so many stories about people who work hard their whole lives and by the time they finally get to retire, they're too old to appreciate it. So I thought I'd go ahead and enjoy the good life while I could!" That might have been a longer speech than I really needed to make, but my new buddy Chris didn't seem to notice.

"Well, we're definitely glad to have you. Are you liking it so far?"

"Yeah!" I nodded. "It's really cute here!"

"Great! That's great! How's your cell phone working here? You know, different phones work differently in different areas. A lot of people think they need a new carrier when they go to a new area, but sometimes all it takes is a new phone. Then you don't have to worry about a new billing system or anything. I have some right over here if you want to take a look. I sell phones for all the major carriers, and I can get you set up right here, right now if you want."

He led me over to the display case under the register. He had about three mid-range phones for each carrier, and not even the phone most people would actually want.

"I don't know," I said reluctantly. "My phone works pretty well. I think I just want a new case for it." I pulled my phone out of my pocket. It had an understated black case that blended in with the phone. It suited me and my style, but for the sake of my investigation, I would get one of the monstrosities Chris was peddling.

He took the phone from my hand and turned it back and forth. He looked almost as disgusted by my black case as I was by his multi-colored ones. "A case like this does not suit a pretty girl like you. Let me show you some that you'll like better."

That I'll like better? I scoffed to myself. *Because I didn't pick that one out in the first place or anything.* But I smiled. "Sure!"

He led me to a wall full of hot pink cell phone cases decorated with flowers and hearts and glitter. They made me gag a little. I was a thirty-four-year-old woman, not a twelve-year-old girl.

"See, aren't these more your style?" he asked.

I smiled tightly. "Yeah, they're much cheerier." At least that was true.

We looked through the cases for a few minutes, him explaining the relative merits of each of them to me. Like the phones, the cases weren't the top of the line, and I knew they wouldn't do much to protect my phone from drops and spills as he said they would. I eventually picked out a case with a large-scale floral print that I could claim vaguely reminded me of a Pucci print. As we went over to the register, I started to worry that I'd dealt with Chris's slime and the ugly phone cases without finding a way to work Mr. Cardosi into the conversation.

Chris insisted on putting the new case on my phone for me. "I can get rid of this old one for you," he said, pulling it across the counter toward himself.

I had paid a pretty penny for that case, and I didn't doubt for a second that he would try to resell it online. "Oh no, I'll keep it. You know, in case I break this one somehow." I giggled for good measure. "I'm such a klutz sometimes!"

"Customer's always right," he said, not really sounding like he meant it.

I took my bag with the new case's packaging in it and turned toward the door. The barbershop was directly in my line of sight, and I saw how to bring Mr. Cardosi up. "Oh!" I said, turning back around.

Chris was right in my face, and he didn't seem to have noticed that I had started speaking. "So, Francesca, since you're new in town, maybe I could take you out sometime and show you around. You know, show you the good places to eat, the best place to get a cup of coffee, where the movie theatre is…"

As if I didn't know the best place to get a cup of coffee. "Um, I don't know." He was uncomfortably close, and I stepped backward. "You know, I'm still just getting settled here and—"

He moved in closer again. "That's exactly why you should let me take you out. I can help you get acquainted with the town!"

"Um, I don't—I don't—" I glanced out the front window at the barbershop. Distraction would be my technique. "Hey, isn't that the shop where the barber who just died worked?"

Chris looked across the street. I used the opportunity to step away again.

"Yeah, that's the place." He laughed.

"What's so funny?" I asked.

"He was just a grouchy old man. I mean, I'm not saying he had it coming, but as angry as that man was, I'm not surprised he pissed someone off enough to murder him."

That was a nauseating statement, especially since Chris was laughing as he said it, but the fact that he knew Mr. Cardosi had been murdered meant that I really needed to ask some more questions.

"He was murdered?" I gasped.

"Oh yeah, you didn't hear?" He sounded excited. "It's all over town. But I guess since you're new here..."

"Do they know who did it?"

"No, not yet," he said. "But it could be anybody. Seriously, dude was *angry*. He was always yelling about something or other. I'd see him outside his store screaming at his customers, telling them to never come back. Now me, I want to make my customers feel special so they want to come back." He gave me a slimy smile, as if he needed to make it more clear that he was coming on to me. When I didn't react, he went back to talking about Mr. Cardosi.

"He came in here once, like a month ago, to buy a phone. The one he had was so old, it still had an *antenna*. I mean, come on, the thing was from, like, the nineties! Anyway, he was in here looking at the new touch screens, and forget apps, he couldn't even make a phone call with one! He kept asking where the keypad was and how he was supposed to dial anybody. It made him so angry, but it was so funny! He just kept poking at it, and every time he'd get close to getting it to do what he wanted, he'd end up hitting the home button or the power button or the volume, then he'd freak out even more. Dude finally just threw the phone on the counter and stormed out. 'I'm taking my business elsewhere!'" Chris said in an impression of Mr. Cardosi.

That was the second Mr. Cardosi impression I'd heard that morning, and I preferred Matty's. Matty's was affectionate. Chris's was just... *rude.*

"I laughed about it for *days!*" he added.

He was still laughing about it. I knew Mr. Cardosi's fits could be comical, but it seemed wrong to laugh about it now that he was dead. Even if I would have considered going out with Chris before, which I wouldn't have, I really wouldn't now. Chris's diatribe had put a bad taste in my mouth, but it had given me the tidbit that Mr. Cardosi had been looking for a new, more modern phone. Maybe that was something useful.

"Well, that's certainly interesting," I said tersely. I was more than ready to get out of there. I looked at my phone briefly. "Oh, look at the time! I really need to get going!" I made for the door.

"What about that date?" Chris asked as I hurried past him.

"I don't think it's going to work out," I said, nearly out the door.

"But why not?" Chris called.

"Oh, just, um..." I glanced around the street. "You're not really my type." I took off down the sidewalk.

Chapter Nine

I hurried down the sidewalk and turned the corner at the end of the block. I didn't know if Chris was watching me walk away—I wasn't about to turn around and look back—but if he was, I wanted to be out of his view as soon as possible. I paused just around the corner to see if I could hear footsteps following me. I couldn't, but I didn't know how likely it was that I would actually be able to hear someone behind me. People always could in the movies, but this was real life, not the latest blockbuster thriller.

I walked for a few more blocks, turning at every corner just in case someone was tailing me. I figured if I was going to investigate Mr. Cardosi's death, I may as well have fun with it. When I arrived at one of the town parks, I made my way to a bench and sat down to text Matty. I assumed he was at work, but I thought I could go ahead and see if he wanted to get together that evening to discuss the case a little more.

I leaned back against the bench to relax while I waited for his response. I wasn't sure if he would be able to respond quickly or not, or if I even merited an immediate response in his book. I gazed around the park. It was one of those cute old parks with a collection of concrete chess tables. My grandfather used to take me there when I was growing up to play chess, but he'd made me practice at home for a long time before he'd let me go to the park and play with his buddies. A scattering of older men were at the chess tables, paired up in competition. A few of them seemed especially serious about it, hitting their chess timers between each move, but most of them were playing more leisurely, seemingly more interested in debating world events than in defeating their opponents.

Hardly a minute later, my phone buzzed. I was pleasantly surprised that Matty had gotten back to me so quickly. He agreed to have a late dinner with me that night after I closed the café. That reminded me I needed to get to work soon. I glanced at the time. I still had a little while. I considered lingering in the park for a while, but then it occurred to me that I also wanted to talk to Mrs. Collins and see if she had any other clues. If I left right away, I could make it back to my neighborhood to talk to her for a little while and still make it to work on time. I might be just a little late, but Sammy would forgive me.

I stood and headed to my street. It wasn't a long walk if you knew the back way. It was counterintuitive, but if I walked through the back of the park, went down the set of stairs in the side of the hill, and took the path around the little pond, I'd pop out just two streets down from my house. I moved quickly, waving at a few of the chess players I recognized as I passed. In no time at all, I was at Mrs. Collins's door.

She didn't have a bell, so I used the heavy, ornate door knocker. There was no answer for quite a while, and I couldn't hear any movement inside the house despite practically putting my ear right up against the door. I was just about to knock again when the door swung open.

Mrs. Collins stood there, her hair done up just so, her lips painted red, her blouse and slacks immaculately pressed. She would have fit in with the finest New York socialites, but that seemed typical of the older generation–they always wanted to look nice, even if they would just be sitting around the house all day. Sometimes I wished my generation had the same attitude, even if I did enjoy being comfortable. She made me feel woefully underdressed, despite the designer labels inside my jeans and black T-shirt. I might have fit in in a New York City office, but I would have looked positively slovenly next to the residents in the Cape Bay retirement home.

"Well, hello, Francesca dear!" Mrs. Collins said warmly, taking my hand in both of hers. "I've just put the kettle on if you'd like to come in for a cup of tea. I'm sorry, I don't keep coffee in the house–I know that's what you'd prefer."

I wondered if putting the kettle on for whoever was at the door was what had taken her so long to answer. I smiled at her warmly. "I'd love that, Mrs. Collins!"

"Well, come on in, dearie!" She stepped aside for me.

Like her, her house was impressively tidy and pulled together. "Neat as a pin," my grandmother would have said.

Mrs. Collins shut the door and shuffled past me down the hall. "If you don't mind, we'll sit in the kitchen. It's difficult for me to carry the tea set into the sitting room anymore."

"Of course!" I said politely.

We walked down the hall and into the brightly lit kitchen.

"Is there anything I can help you with?" I asked.

"No, no, dear, it'll just be a minute," she replied.

She certainly was fond of calling me "dear." As I sat at the table, it occurred to me that she hadn't yet inquired as to the reason for my visit. She must have just been so happy to have a visitor that she didn't care about the reason for their arrival. I watched her move around the kitchen, gathering tea cups and sugar and tea bags.

She arranged it all neatly on a silver tea tray even though we would just be sitting at the table. When the kettle whistled, she added it to the tray and shuffled over to the table, dismissing my continued offers of assistance. She carefully poured tea for each of us and took a sip before speaking.

"So, Francesca, to what do I owe the pleasure of this visit?"

I decided to plead a need for commiseration. I sighed deeply. "Well, Mrs. Collins, you know, Mr. Cardosi's death has just been weighing on me. I know you said on the day he..." I paused for effect. "The day he passed away that you'd spent a lot of time with him, so I felt like you, of all people, would be able to chat with me about him."

"Oh yes, dear. So sad, isn't it? And him so young yet."

I hadn't really thought of Mr. Cardosi as *young*, but I supposed if you were pushing eighty, as Mrs. Collins was, Mr. Cardosi's late sixties did seem rather youthful.

I nodded. "You were close to him?" Chris the Cell Phone Guy had shared freely after just a simple question, and I hoped that technique would work similarly well with Mrs. Collins.

"I was! That's why it's been so hard for me. You know, so many of my friends are passing now. Your mother, then Gino Cardosi. And death comes in threes, you know. I just keep waiting for who will be next." She shook her head sadly.

I looked at her sympathetically. I wished she hadn't mentioned my mother, but I supposed it had been a bad couple of months for our block, and she was entitled to be sad about it too.

As I'd hoped, she continued talking after a brief pause. "You know, lately, I'd been going over in the evenings to help Gino practice courting a lady." The shock must have shown on my face because Mrs. Collins rushed to continue. "Oh no, no, no, dear. He wasn't courting *me*. It was someone else—he wouldn't tell me who. But he hadn't dated anyone since his Carolina—that was Matteo's mother—passed away twenty-five years ago, and he was dreadfully out of practice. We just went over basic things—pulling a chair out for a lady, helping her with her coat, how to not make a mess of himself when eating spaghetti Bolognese. I helped him pick out some outfits to wear out to dinner with her that made him look like the respectable businessman he was."

I got the feeling from the way Mrs. Collins was talking that she wished she really had been the one Mr. Cardosi was courting—if he was actually courting anyone at all. I reminded myself of Mrs. Collins's tendency to exaggerate and Matty's confidence that his dad was largely a loner. It seemed entirely possible that Mrs. Collins had invited herself over to Mr. Cardosi's with the intention of making him over as a suitor for herself, or some other watered-down version of what she had told me. But then something she said caught my attention.

"Apparently the lady he was seeing, despite being a more mature woman like myself, was quite technological. She wanted to be able to—oh, what is it you young people call that? When you type to each other on your phones?"

"Text?" I prompted.

"Yes! Text! Apparently she wanted to be able to text messages to Gino, but his cell phone didn't do that, and he wanted to get a new one that would let him do that. He went to that awful place across from his barbershop, but the young man who works there was quite rude to him. Gino didn't buy anything."

So maybe there was something to Mrs. Collins's story after all. I glanced at the clock on the wall and realized I needed to get to the coffee shop. I swallowed the rest of my tea. "Mrs. Collins, I've had such a lovely time with you, but I need to get to work. Thank you for the tea." I rose from my chair so she wouldn't be able to delay me by starting more stories.

She sighed and put everything back on the tea tray. "Well, I do appreciate you coming, dear. You know you're welcome here any time. Watching you grow up was always such a joy. You know, Mr. Collins and I were never able to have children, so having you across the street was almost like having one of our own grandchildren there."

I stopped and looked at her. I had never known that she felt that way. I gave her a hug. "Thank you, Mrs. Collins. That's so sweet of you." When I pulled away, I thought I saw tears in her eyes. After being home for over a month, I was finally realizing how deep my roots ran in this town.

"Well, dear, it's the truth."

I smiled and noticed the tea tray on the table. "Let me carry that over to the sink for you." I put the rest of the dishes on the tray and carried it to the counter so she wouldn't have to. I gave her one more hug and hurried off to the café.

Chapter Ten

"Have fun at the beach?" Sammy asked as I walked into the backroom of the café. Her normally pale face was flushed bright red from working over steaming coffee all morning.

I smiled. "Yeah, it was nice! I got to get my feet wet, dig my toes in the sand, relax a little. I took off when the tourists started coming in."

It was a common sentiment in seaside towns: tourists leave the beach when the tide starts coming in; locals leave when the tourists start coming in. It wasn't that we didn't like the tourists—we really did. It was fun getting to meet new people all the time, and the boon to the local economy was great. By the end of the summer, though, we were ready to turn back into the sleepy town we were the other nine months of the year.

"I'm surprised there were any tourists left to go out to the beach—it seemed like they were all here," Sammy said.

"So it's been busy!"

Sammy turned from the dishes she was scrubbing, and I noticed her normally loose wisps of hair were plastered to her face. "Busy is an understatement."

I couldn't help but laugh at her deadpan delivery. I took my apron off its hook and dropped it over my head. I poked my head out into the café as I tied the apron's sash behind my back. Becky was wiping down the counter, her red curls a little extra frizzy from the heat and humidity. Several people were scattered among the tables and chairs, but it looked as if the rush had mostly died down.

"I can take care of that if you want to get out of here," I said, gesturing at Sammy's dishes.

"That's okay. I'm almost done." Sammy wasn't the type to leave a job unfinished, even if someone was offering to take it over for her.

I grabbed a rag and went out to the front to wipe down tables and straighten up. I could always find something to fiddle around with, whether it was cleaning things or moving things around or preparing food. Sammy finished the dishes and went home, and Amanda, another of our teenage part-timers, came in to relieve Becky. The afternoon just got slower. By mid-afternoon, we had taken care of everything that needed to be done and we didn't have a single customer, so I let Amanda go home after she promised to come back if things picked up and I needed her.

I stood behind the counter, glancing around the empty café. Days like this always made me nervous. They were few and far between, but they always made me worry that business was slowing down overall and soon we'd have to close. I knew it was ridiculous, especially as busy as Sammy said it had been during the morning, but I worried all the same.

I went in the back to get the notebook and pens I'd purchased and took them back to the front. I leaned over the counter and wrote down everything I'd learned that morning—everything I'd talked about with slimy Chris and old Mrs. Collins. I included my impressions about my conversations with each of them. I wanted to remember what I'd thought in the moment about Mrs. Collins's possible exaggerations and Chris's obnoxious offensiveness. With the small size of the notebook, I quickly filled up each page and found myself wishing I'd gotten a bigger notebook, even if it was somewhat less portable.

I finished my notes just as the late afternoon "rush" got started. Apparently everyone who was going to come in that day had come during the morning because, while I had to hustle, I never got to the point where I had to call Amanda back in. It quickly slowed back down, and I was left with a few pairs of customers lingering over their drinks. I felt a little bit guilty that things had been so hectic for Sammy but so easy for me. After the last of the customers left, I wiped everything down again and waited for closing time.

I was in the backroom five minutes before closing, rearranging items on the shelves, when I heard the jingle of the bell over the door. I walked out into the café, a little annoyed that I'd have to make someone a drink when everything was already clean and put away. At the same time, I recognized that was my fault for cleaning up early. A smile spread across my face when I saw Matty, still looking handsome in his work clothes.

"Hey!" I said cheerily.

"Hey yourself!" he replied. "You about ready to get something to eat?"

"Yeah, I just have to lock up." I glanced at the clock on the wall. There were still a couple of minutes left before the official closing time. To most people, that would be inconsequential, but I had spent so long working beside my grandparents and being told that you have to be open when you say you're going to be open, I wasn't sure if I would physically be able to turn the key in the lock before precisely closing time. I hesitated. "Well, in two minutes."

Matty looked at the clock and laughed. "Ghosts of your grandparents keeping you from closing shop thirty seconds early?"

I shrugged with a smile. Even after spending most of the last fifteen years apart, he knew me too well. We stood and watched the clock tick down until the minute hand was precisely lined up with the twelve, then I walked over to the door and turned the lock.

I smiled at Matty. "Okay, now we can go."

He gestured at me. "Might want to take that apron off. Otherwise they might try to put you to work at dinner."

I rolled my eyes at his bad joke as I walked to the backroom and took off my apron. I grabbed my purse and headed for the door, turning lights out as I went. Matty followed me out and waited as I locked up.

"So what's for dinner?" I asked.

"I was thinking the little Mexican place down on the beach?" he suggested.

"Sounds good to me," I replied. "I could go for a margarita about now."

"No tequila shots?" Matty joked.

"I didn't say no tequila," I teased back. "I just said I wanted a margarita. We can work our way up to straight tequila."

Matty laughed as we walked down the sidewalk toward the beach. It was a warm night, with just the slightest breeze blowing out to the ocean. The sun was sinking below the horizon behind us as we approached the water.

"You want to sit outside?" Matty asked when we arrived at the restaurant with its deck that stretched out over the water.

"Definitely." The full moon would be rising momentarily, and there were few things I loved more than watching the moon reflected over the water.

Matty gave our request to the hostess, and she escorted us out onto the deck. Something about that evening must have made all the businesses on the beach slow, because we were the only ones out there, and the inside of the restaurant was sparsely populated. I tried to remember if there was a concert or something in a nearby town that was luring everyone away, but nothing came to mind. Matty pulled my chair out for me then went around to his side of the table as the waitress appeared, chips and salsa in hand, to take our drink orders.

"Margarita on the rocks, please," I told her.

Matty hesitated for a moment, giving me a look that I knew meant he was toying with the idea of jumping straight to tequila, but he ordered a beer instead. We studied our menus as the waitress disappeared to get our drinks.

"I don't know what I want," Matty muttered. "I want everything!"

"Hungry much?" I asked with a laugh.

"I haven't eaten since lunch." He groaned. "I'm starving!"

"Eat some chips!" I said, shoving the bowl across the table toward him.

Matty grabbed two and shoved them in his mouth.

"Charming," I said.

"I told you I'm hungry," Matty said around the chips.

I laughed at his obviously unnecessary crudeness. It was juvenile humor, but sometimes it's fun to be juvenile. The waitress reappeared with our drinks. That was one thing I liked about that place—they actually made your drinks and brought them out to you quickly. I couldn't stand it when you ordered a drink and for some reason it took twenty minutes to get to your table. I gave the waitress our orders then sipped our drinks as she left.

"So," I said, figuring we needed to get down to business. "I went and talked to Cell

Phone Guy—his name is Chris Tompson—and Mrs. Collins today—"

Matty cut me off, reaching across the table. "Please, Franny, can we not talk about my dad just yet? Let's just sit and enjoy each other's company for a while, okay? We can talk about anything else."

I smiled. Matty and I hadn't just sat and talked in ages, certainly not since I'd been back in town.

"Sure," I said. Out of the corner of my eye, I saw the moon starting to peek up over the water. It sounded like a perfect way to spend the evening.

Chapter Eleven

We lingered a while over dinner. I never did switch to tequila, but I did have more than one margarita. The moon was stunning over the water. It was large and full and made the night unusually bright. Matty and I chatted about our lives since high school and how we ended up back in Cape Bay.

Matty had gone away to college too, but he moved back right afterward because he didn't want to leave his dad all alone. He'd had a couple girlfriends, one of them pretty serious. She had wanted to get married, but Matty wasn't ready, and they broke up.

I filled him in on what had happened with my ex-fiancé. He'd heard about it, of course, because once my mother told one person that her daughter's engagement was off, the whole town knew—that was the way the rumor mill worked in a small town. I gave him the unexaggerated version of the story, though, not the one that had been built up through retellings by people who weren't there and didn't actually know. The woman he'd left me for wasn't a model, I didn't catch them in bed together, I didn't throw all his belongings out the window. I told him the boring but true version—he left me, and my heart was broken.

We had long since finished eating and were nursing our third round of drinks when our conversation about our personal lives wound down.

Matty sighed. "I guess we should go ahead and talk about my dad." He gestured at the inside of the restaurant, where only a few customers were left and the waitstaff was wiping down tables. "They're going to want us out of here pretty soon."

I was enjoying my time with Matty so much, I had almost forgotten what had brought us out to dinner that night. I pulled my notebook out of my bag and flipped through the pages I'd filled at the café, refreshing my memory about my conversations.

"You took notes?" Matty asked wryly.

I glanced up, the very picture of seriousness. "Yes, yes, I did." I looked back down at my notes.

Matty chuckled and took a drink of his beer.

Satisfied I knew the points I wanted to cover, I flipped my notebook closed again. "Do you know anything about your dad shopping for a new cell phone?"

"No. Why?" Matty said slowly.

I gave him a brief rundown of my conversations with Chris the Cell Phone Guy and Mrs. Collins. That both of them mentioned Mr. Cardosi was looking for a new cell phone made me think there might actually be something to it. Matty listened thoughtfully.

After a long pause, he spoke. "The weekend before he died, he mentioned that he was going to Plymouth so he could go to one of those big box stores—I can't remember which one. I didn't understand what he needed to do out there, but I guess if he wanted a cell phone and didn't want to go to the cell phone shop—and you know he wouldn't go back there after he got into an argument with that guy—I guess he might have been going to get a cell phone." Matty looked thoughtful. "I wonder why he didn't tell me."

I shrugged, then something occurred to me. "If the thing Mrs. Collins said about your dad dating someone was true, maybe he was worried how you'd feel about it."

Matty played with his beer bottle. He sighed. "I just—Mom died so long ago. I would have been happy for him if he'd told me he found someone."

"You know how parents are. My mom talked about her 'friend' John for years, and every time I'd ask, she denied that there was anything between them. But the way she smiled when she talked about him said otherwise. They just want to protect us."

"I guess you're right," Matty said quietly. He shook his head. "I just wish I'd known."

We sat for a few minutes, both lost in our thoughts about our parents.

Finally Matty glanced up and gestured inside the restaurant with his beer bottle. "We should probably get going."

The other customers were gone, and the servers were hovering just inside, looking at us every once in a while as though they didn't want to pressure us too much even if they were ready to go home.

"Yeah, I guess we should."

Matty caught our waitress's eye, and she brought over the check. I reached for my purse, but before I could get my wallet out, Matty had slid his credit card into the folder and passed it back to the waitress.

"What was that?" I asked indignantly.

"Me paying for our dinner?" Matty answered.

"I can pay for myself. And if anyone's going to be paying for anyone, I should be paying for you because I'm the one who suggested dinner."

Matty shrugged. "Too late."

I looked at him through narrowed eyes. "Well, I'm paying next time."

He shrugged again, this time with a twinkle in his eye. "We'll see."

I had a feeling I'd have to fight to pay.

"You know, it's only fair that I pay," Matty said. "You've treated me at the café twice in the past two days."

"That's different."

"How?"

"It just is." I didn't really have a reason except that I ran the café and could give out free food and drinks to anyone at any time, but Matty was going out of his way to pay for my dinner.

Matty didn't bother arguing with me anymore. He just signed the check when the waitress brought it back. We left quickly so the staff could finish cleaning up and go home.

"Where's your car?" I asked as we started up the street toward the café. Matty's house was on the other side of town. It was a quick drive but far enough that I knew he wouldn't have walked to the café.

"I actually parked at my dad's house," he said. "I didn't see any reason to pay for parking when his place is just around the corner."

"Well, good," I replied cheerily. "I'll have company on my walk home."

Matty scoffed. "You think I'd let you walk home alone at this time of night?"

I looked at him, surprised by both what he said and how forcefully he said it. "You think I can't take care of myself? I lived in New York for twelve years! I think I can handle sleepy Cape Bay. It's not like this is a dangerous place!" Matty didn't say anything, and I realized what I had just said. "Oh... um, I mean, usually, um–"I couldn't believe how badly I'd stuck my foot in my mouth.

"It's okay," he offered. "I would have felt the same way before. I do have manners, you know." He chuckled softly.

"Thanks." I sighed, relieved that my gaffe hadn't upset Matty too much. "And sorry. I should have thought before I said that."

"It's okay." He rubbed the back of my shoulder. "Really."

We walked on in silence, enjoying each other's company and the peace of the night. After a few minutes, we turned onto our street–well, my street and Matty's old street.

"What are you going to do with your dad's house?" I asked.

"I don't know yet," Matty said. "It's paid for. I could sell it and put the money into my own place. Or I could take a cue from you and sell my place and move into his. It'd be nice to not have a mortgage."

"Hey! Then there'd be two young people on the street!"

Matty laughed. "That is true." We were walking up to his dad's house. "You want to come in and see if we can find anything about that cell phone? There wasn't one in his personal effects that they returned to me, so the old one or the new one's got to be inside somewhere, right?"

"Unless..." My newly discovered investigator's mind went off.

"Unless whoever killed him took it," Matty finished. "Either way, we should find out."

I agreed, and we headed into Mr. Cardosi's house to hunt for his cell phone or some evidence of it. Matty unlocked the door and flipped on the light. We stood in the foyer, taking in the space.

"Where do we start?" I asked after a minute.

"Anywhere we didn't already look." Matty looked around. "I'll start with the bedroom. Do you want to come with me or look somewhere else?"

I glanced around the entrance. "I'll start out here."

"All righty," Matty said and headed into Mr. Cardosi's bedroom.

A few jackets hung on hooks by the door, and a couple of shopping bags were on the floor beneath them. Wanting to start small, I stuck my hand in one of the jacket pockets and immediately closed it around a solid plastic rectangle. Not believing it could be that easy, I pulled my hand out slowly and turned the rectangle over. Sure enough, it was a brand-new smartphone. Not high-end but definitely a touch screen and definitely no antenna.

"Matty?" I called.

"Just a second, I'm just going through his nightstand."

"I found it."

There was a pause. "What?"

"I found it."

Another pause. Matty appeared in the bedroom door, an incredulous look on his face. "You found it? Already? What, was it in the first place you looked?"

I nodded, grinning. "Sure was!"

Matty took the two steps over to me with his hand out. I handed him the phone. He looked at it slowly.

"What do you know?" he said quietly. "He did buy one."

I wondered if it bothered him that his dad had bought a phone, supposedly so that he could text the woman he was dating, without breathing a word of it to Matty. He pushed the home button. Nothing happened. He pushed the power button. Nothing. He pushed it again, holding it down for several seconds. I saw his eyebrows go up, and he turned it around for me to see the screen light up.

"He always kept the old one off too," he said. "Said he wanted to make sure it was charged up in case he needed it in an emergency. I told him he could just charge it each night, but he thought that was ridiculous. 'Batteries should last longer than that!'" Matty slipped into his impression of his dad again, even shaking his fist for good measure. He chuckled softly as he thought about his dad.

I moved closer so we could look at the screen together. "Has he been texting anyone?" Since that was why he bought the phone, it seemed like the most obvious place to start.

Matty opened the text messaging app. It was empty.

"Call log?" I suggested.

Matty fumbled around briefly, trying to figure out how to see the call history. It was a different model phone from his, and it wasn't the most intuitive design. My phone was different too, so I wasn't any help. Finally he found it. All the calls were to one number. Matty read it out loud.

"Do you know whose number that is?" I asked.

"Nope."

"Let's call it!" I suggested.

He looked at the time on the phone then looked at me. "It's almost midnight."

"So that's a no?" I tried to look as serious as possible even though I obviously knew it was way too late to call.

Matty looked at me skeptically then laughed after he realized I was joking. I clearly wasn't doing a good job of looking serious.

"We'll call tomorrow," he said.

"Oh-kay," I said dramatically. I had gotten relatively little sleep the night before and was getting a little slap-happy.

Matty chuckled again. "I think you might need to get home and get to bed."

"Yeah, probably," I admitted.

Matty started to put the phone away.

"No, wait!" I put my hand on his arm to stop him. My investigator brain had kicked in again. I reached for my purse, which I had dropped on the floor when we came in. "I want to copy that number and the call times down."

I pulled out my notebook and wrote it all down as Matty held the phone patiently, rubbing his finger on the screen every few seconds to keep it from going to sleep. There were only a few calls, so it didn't take long to get it all.

"Okay, thanks," I said, slapping the notebook closed and stuffing it back in my bag.

"Can I take you home now?" Matty asked.

"It's just two doors down. I think I'll be okay."

Matty just looked at me.

"Okay!" I said, giving in. "Are you trying to make me feel helpless or something today?"

"I'm *trying* to be a gentleman," Matty replied, shepherding me out the door and locking it behind us.

"Well, I can't really argue with that, can I?" I was used to being independent, but it's not as if he was patting my head and telling me a pretty girl like me shouldn't be worrying her little head about something as big and complicated as a coffee shop. I just wasn't used to someone—a man especially—being so considerate. My ex-fiancé certainly hadn't been.

We cut across the neighbor's lawn on the way to my house on the other side. I unlocked my door then turned to look at Matty.

"Well, thanks for dinner," I said.

"It was my pleasure," Matty replied.

"You want to get together tomorrow and try to call that number?"

"Sure. Do you have to work?"

"Only a couple hours at close." The next day was Saturday which, weirdly, was one of our slowest days, at least during the summer. Since all the rentals rolled over on Saturdays, not many people had the opportunity to come in. The renters from the previous week were too busy packing up and heading out of town, and the next week's renters hadn't found us yet. As a result, we usually broke the day's shifts down so Sammy and I only had to worry about opening and closing, and some of the more established part-timers shared duty during the day.

"So maybe we can grab some lunch then see if we can figure out who my dad was calling?"

"Sounds good!" I replied.

We stood there, looking at each other awkwardly, for a few seconds, as if we were both waiting to see if the other had something more to say.

"Well, I guess I'll see you tomorrow," I said finally.

"Yeah." Matty stood there for a second then hugged me.

It was... strange. Hugging him wasn't unusual, but the nature of that hug seemed out of the ordinary. It seemed as though he held me maybe a little bit tighter and a little bit longer than normal. It wasn't bad, just... different. When he let me go, I opened the door and stepped inside. Matty gave me a little wave.

"Good night," he said before he headed back across the lawn to his car parked at his dad's.

"Good night." I watched him walk away then closed the door. I stood there for a minute and wondered if maybe there was something more to that hug than simple friendship.

Chapter Twelve

I knew I was tired, but I didn't feel like going to bed yet. I went into the kitchen and poured myself a glass of wine. The house was quiet. So very, very quiet. I wandered through the first floor, flipping lights on as I went. The lights made the stillness feel a little less ominous.

I opened the door to my grandparents' bedroom. I had never thought of my mother as a particularly sentimental person, but I supposed she had been since she'd never moved into their bedroom after they both passed away. She hadn't really cleaned it out. Their clothes were still hanging neatly in the closet, their knickknacks still arranged on the dresser.

I picked up a bottle of my grandmother's perfume and sprayed it in the air. Even after all these years, it still smelled just like her. My grandfather's cologne was the same way. I sat on the edge of their bed, closed my eyes, and breathed them in. On the one hand, it felt as if they had just died a minute ago, but on the other, I felt every one of the eleven years since their passing. They'd died within months of each other, my grandmother from a quick-moving pancreatic cancer and my grandfather from heart failure in his sleep. Losing them in such quick succession had been hard on my mother and me, but my grandfather hadn't been the same since my grandmother's passing, and we knew he was ready to be with her again.

I opened my eyes and looked around the room. Maybe I should move down there. Clean out their things, give it a fresh coat of paint. There was no sense in leaving it as a museum or treating the whole house as if it were frozen in time, a tomb for ghosts to lurk about in. I supposed that meant I'd need to go through my mother's things as well. Maybe I should go through the whole house. Spruce it up some, "young" it up, make it a place that a thirty-something single woman would live in. That sounded like a plan. Although the house still seemed dreadfully quiet. Maybe I needed a pet. A dog or a cat. Despite all of my grandfather's wonderful traits, he had adamantly refused to allow a pet in the house, no matter how much I'd begged and pleaded. But there was no reason I had to keep it "people only" anymore. If I wanted a pet, I could get a pet. It wasn't as though I had a job that kept me away for long hours each day—I could arrange my schedule at the café however I needed to so that I could come home to take care of Fido or Fluffy. That settled it. I was getting a pet. I would go to the shelter to find the perfect critter to love just as soon as I could.

I went upstairs and got ready for bed. I lay down and thought about what I would turn this room into when I moved downstairs into the master bedroom. Maybe an office. Or an exercise studio. I had my mother's old room to do something with, so I could make one room into an office and the other into an exercise studio. Or a guest room. I could make one of the rooms into a guest room. Sooner or later one of my friends from New York would want to come up and spend some time at the beach. I thought for a while about how I could redecorate and possibly renovate the house. I wasn't falling asleep. I let my mind wander, and it wasn't long before it drifted to my investigation of Mr. Cardosi's death.

I thought about that phone number. Which of us would call it—Matty or me? We shouldn't try to call from Mr. Cardosi's cell phone, should we? What if the person recognized his number? If it was the murderer, wouldn't that tip him off that we were on his trail? So we should call from a different number. One of our cell phones? What if that could be traced? What if the murderer just did an online search for the number and it turned up Matty's or my information?

I sat straight up in bed. If the murderer—or whoever the number belonged to, I was getting ahead of myself assuming it was the murderer's number—could find out online who called him, why couldn't I search for him? I got up and grabbed my laptop from my dresser. I was antsy for it to hurry up and turn on and for the browser to load. Slowness that normally didn't bother me was driving me nuts.

Finally, I got the browser loaded and the search engine pulled up. I typed in the number I had copied off the call log on Mr. Cardosi's phone. The number was for Mary Ellen's Souvenirs and Gifts, the local souvenir shop. It was just down the street from my café. When we were kids, Mary Ellen Chapman, the owner of the shop, was just about the only adult in town who we were allowed to call by her first name. She'd said it was silly for us to call her Mrs. Chapman when her first name was right on the front of the store. Of course, at our parents' insistence, we had to call her "Miss Mary Ellen," not just "Mary Ellen," but still, that made her instantly cool in our eyes. She was younger than our parents too—probably not as much as it seemed at the time because parents are decidedly ancient in their children's eyes—but her youth made her even cooler to us.

As far as I could remember, she had been married once when she was young. Her husband had passed away, leaving her a chunk of money that was more than enough for her to move to Cape Bay, buy a house, and set up her souvenir shop. She didn't just sell kitschy Cape Bay memorabilia—she also sold a lot of handmade jewelry, clothing, and art from local artisans, including herself.

She was a knitter and made sweaters that I swore were every bit as nice as the ones I could buy in a department store. Her shop was a surprisingly good place to go to get gifts for people.

I wondered whether Mary Ellen was the woman Mr. Cardosi had been seeing. I'd seen her around town since I'd been back, and while she was getting older, she still seemed youthful and spunky. She didn't really seem like the type who would be interested in Mr. Cardosi and all his grumpy argumentativeness, but what did I know? If he'd been spending time with Mrs. Collins to polish some of his rough edges, maybe he was a bigger softie than I'd thought. Mary Ellen was probably old enough that she could be considered "mature," as Mrs. Collins had referred to her, and she certainly seemed like she knew how to text. It was a possibility.

I put my laptop away and crawled back into bed. Instead of calling the number tomorrow, I'd suggest to Matty that we just go over to the souvenir shop and talk to Mary Ellen in person. I'd be able to get a better read on her if I could see her while we talked to her. I couldn't rule out the possibility that she was the murderer, as unlikely as it seemed. I drifted off to sleep as I planned out what I would say to her when we saw her.

I woke up late the next day—no surprise given that it had been after two when I'd finally fallen asleep. My text message alert finally roused me. I rolled over and looked at my phone. The message was from Matty.

What do you want for lunch?

Was it lunchtime already? I looked at the time. It was definitely pushing noon. I hadn't slept that late in ages.

I *don't know,* I texted back. *I need to get up and get a shower before we do anything.*

I had barely gotten out of bed when Matty's reply came in. He must have been waiting for my reply.

You're not up yet?? Lazy! You better hurry. My fingers are getting itchy to call this number!

I realized I hadn't told Matty what I'd discovered about the phone number last night.

Don't call it! I texted back. I *have something to tell you about it.*

Ok, but you better hurry...

Matty seemed as though he was in a playful mood. I hurried into the shower and heard another text come in. I thought about jumping out to see what it said, but I didn't really feel like cleaning up the water that would pour all over the bathroom floor in the process. Instead, I grabbed it as soon as I was done.

I'm going to head over. I'll be at my dad's whenever you're ready.

Matty's house was so close by, I needed to hurry if I didn't want him to be waiting forever. I reached into my closet, instinctively grabbing a black shirt. But I stopped myself. Black seemed so New York, and I wasn't in New York anymore. Black once in a while wasn't a bad thing, but I didn't need to wear it every day. I went across the hall to my mother's room. I was lucky that she had stayed stylish and my size. I pulled out a pretty cornflower top I had always admired. I slid it over my head and looked at myself in the mirror. It suited me as it had my mother. It brought out the flecks of blue we both had in our eyes.

I finished getting ready and headed over to Mr. Cardosi's house. I rang the bell and looked around while I waited for Matty to open the door. The house was in decent shape—new paint, well maintained. The flower beds needed some attention, but I supposed that was up to Matty, or his real estate agent if he decided to sell the place. The door opened.

"Hey!" Matty said exuberantly. "You look nice! You're wearing a color!"

I glanced at my shirt. I wasn't sure if I was more surprised that he'd noticed that my shirt was blue or that I usually wore black. "Thanks. You look nice too," I said, somewhat automatically.

"This?" He gestured at his T-shirt and shorts. "Your standards must have dropped since you left the city."

I laughed. Maybe his outfit wasn't the most stylish, but his hair looked good and I kind of liked his scruffy, unshaven weekend look.

"You ready to go?" Matty asked before I could say anything else.

"Sure, where are we going?"

"I have a craving for lobster rolls," he replied. "Sound good?"

My mouth started watering as soon as he said it. "Yes!" From the way Matty laughed at me, I probably sounded a little too enthusiastic.

"Well, let's go," he said, leading the way down the sidewalk.

There was only one place to go for lobster rolls in Cape Bay. Well, there was more than one place to go, but the locals knew only one place was worth going to. Sandy's Seafood Shack was pretty much the best place on the beach for any New England seafood—lobster rolls, fresh lobster, clam chowder in the winter. Some other places got by on the strength of the tourist trade and plenty kept lobster rolls on their menus just because they knew people would order it, but Sandy's was pretty much the be all, end all for those of us who lived there year-round.

Sandy's was way at the end of the beach, about a fifteen-minute walk from my house. One of my favorite things about Cape Bay, at least the part where I lived, was that I could pretty much walk anywhere. I had a driver's license and a car, but between growing up in Cape Bay, going to school in Boston, and living in New York for so long, walking everywhere was second nature to me. It felt weird to drive anywhere that took less than thirty minutes to walk to. On our walk, we chit-chatted about the neighborhood, how things had changed in town since we were kids, and our old friends from growing up. We were at Sandy's in practically no time.

Lots of people assumed that one of the married couple who opened Sandy's was actually named Sandy. Both of them were called that on a regular basis. Now that their kids ran the place, they also got called Sandy all the time by well-meaning tourists. Whenever somebody asked, "Are you Sandy?" whoever was being asked would just smile and say, "Sure am!" The name was actually a nickname for the owners' dog though. Her name had been Josie, but she liked to roll on the beach and get all sandy. Josie/Sandy had long since passed away and been replaced by other dogs, all of whom they continued to name Sandy. I think they were on Sandy Five by then.

As we settled into our lobster rolls, Matty asked me what I had wanted to tell him about the phone number we'd found.

I finished chewing and put my lobster roll down. "It's Mary Ellen's number."

Matty about choked. "What?"

"Mary Ellen Chapman," I clarified. "It's the souvenir shop's number."

"You think my dad was dating Mary Ellen?" Matty seemed more surprised than I'd expected.

"Well, I don't know if he was dating her, but that's whose number he was calling. I figured we could just go over there and talk to her instead of calling."

"Mary Ellen Chapman," Matty repeated, seemingly not hearing what I'd said. He shook his head slowly, and I thought I saw a bit of a smile on his face.

"Why do you seem so... I don't know, surprised? I mean, she's younger than your dad, but not that much. She was already running the souvenir shop when we were kids."

"No, I know," Matty said. "It's just—" He stopped talking and stared into space a little.

"It's just what?" I took a sip of my soda. Soda felt right with lobster rolls.

"It's just—" he repeated. "Well, I had a little bit of a crush on Mary Ellen growing up."

Chapter Thirteen

It was my turn to choke. I narrowly managed to avoid spitting soda all over Matty. "You what?" Somehow it seemed completely ludicrous to me that Matty had had a crush on Mary Ellen.

He shrugged, blushing a little. "You know, she was young and pretty and—what's so funny?"

I was giggling uncontrollably without really being sure why.

"Seriously, what's so funny?" Matty asked again, starting to giggle himself.

"I don't—I don't know!" I gasped through my giggles. "There's just something—something so funny about you having a crush on her and then your dad dating her twenty years later!" I was laughing so hard I was shaking the table.

"I don't know if you laughing so hard about it should make me feel bad or not." Matty laughed.

"It shouldn't make you feel any particular way. It's just—it struck me as funny." I was getting my giggles under control, taking big deep breaths to calm myself down.

I gradually managed to stop laughing, and we finished our lunch. We agreed to head over to the souvenir shop right afterward. I left the table to go wash my hands, and when I came back, Matty was standing by the table.

"Ready to go?" I asked.

"Ready to go," he replied.

We walked toward the front of the restaurant, where the cash register was.

"Did you grab the check from the table?" I asked him.

"Yup, and paid," he said, walking toward the door instead of the register.

"What!"

Matty grinned as he pushed the door open. "You got up. I paid. Too late again."

I glanced at the girl at the register, and she nodded and said, "Yup, he already paid."

I scowled at Matty as I walked through the door. "You were supposed to let me pay this time."

"That was something you decided," Matty said. "I never agreed to it."

"But it's not fair for you to always pay!"

"Fair only counts in horseshoes and—no, that's wrong," Matty said, interrupting himself. "The point is, I don't care. I invited you out to lunch. I paid. Simple as that."

"But I invited you last night and you paid!"

"Yeah, you're right," he said.

"So shouldn't I pay today?"

"Apparently not."

I glared at the back of his head as he walked down the sidewalk. Eventually he turned around and looked at me.

"You coming?" he asked.

"Are you going to let me pay next time?"

"Is that the only way you'll come with me?"

"Yes," I said.

"Then yes, you can pay next time." He muttered something else as I walked toward him.

"What was that?" I asked.

"What was what?" He had an innocent look that gave away how guilty he was.

"What did you say after you said I could pay next time?"

He threw his arm around my shoulders and leaned his head toward me. "I *definitely* didn't say that there was no way you were paying."

He had a big grin. I knew I wouldn't win that battle, at least not that day, so I just shook my head.

It was about a ten-minute walk to Mary Ellen's store. It was a relatively warm day but not too humid, so the walk wasn't bad.

"So how are we going to do this?" I asked when we got to the block with Mary Ellen's store.

"You're the investigator," Matty said.

"I'm not an investigator," I scoffed.

"You're the one who's been doing the investigating?" Matty corrected, a question in his voice, seemingly unsure how I wanted to categorize my inquiries. "Seems like you've done well so far with Cell Phone Guy and Mrs. Collins, so I don't see why you shouldn't take the lead here too."

It made me nervous, but his confidence in me felt good. I thought about how to approach Mary Ellen as we got closer. With Chris the Cell Phone Guy and Mrs. Collins, I'd kept my cards pretty close to my chest, but I felt as though it might be better to be a little more open with Mary Ellen. We got to the store, and Matty opened the door for me, jingling the bell above the door. Mary Ellen appeared from the back as we stepped inside.

"Hello!" she called before she had quite seen us. She gasped when she did. "Fran! Matt! What brings the two of you in today?"

I saw Matt look at me, so I smiled and stepped forward. "Hi, Mary Ellen!" I did my best to sound light-hearted and happy. "How are you today?"

"I'm good, I'm good," she replied.

She really did look good for her age. If I didn't know better, I would have thought she were ten years younger than she really was. Her clothes were still fashionable, and she either had amazing genes or she dyed her hair to keep it a warm chestnut. She stood behind the counter, looking completely comfortable in her skin.

"How are you?" she asked.

"I'm good," I said, smiling. I walked over to her, Matty close behind me. "I'm wondering if you could help us with something."

She wrinkled her forehead and frowned slightly. "I'd be happy to, if I can."

"Matty—"I needed to stop calling him Matty, at least when I was talking to other people. People had to think I sounded eight years old when I called him that when everybody else just called him Matt. "*Matt* and I were taking care of some of his dad's things the other day, and we found his cell phone. We noticed there were quite a few calls to your number."

She blushed and looked at the counter. She took a deep breath, and when she looked back up, tears were welling up in her eyes. "Gino—your dad," she said, looking at Matty—Matt. "Your dad and I had been spending some time together before he passed away."

"You were dating?" I prompted.

She looked back down. "Well, I wouldn't say—I suppose—it was casual. I was—I was also seeing another man." Her voice got very quiet as she said the last part.

My independent spirit reared up, not wanting Mary Ellen to feel bad for dating two men at once. As long as she wasn't cheating on one or the other, there was nothing to be ashamed of.

"Were you exclusive with either of them?" I asked. "I mean, did either of them think you were?"

"Oh, heavens no!" she said quickly. "No, no, I would never do that. See one man behind another's back, I mean. I suppose I would be exclusive with a gentleman under some circumstances, but I haven't since my husband passed. I haven't felt like I wanted to tie myself down that way again. No, they knew about each other. They despised each other, but they knew about each other."

I nodded sympathetically. I understood her wanting to maintain her freedom, and I wanted her to feel as though she could continue to confide in me. I glanced at Matt, who was making himself busy inspecting some magnets emblazoned with

"Cape Bay." My ears had latched onto Mary Ellen's comment that Mr. Cardosi and her other suitor had despised each other. It seemed like the right moment to bring the conversation around to Mr. Cardosi's cause of death.

I lowered my voice and leaned across the counter toward Mary Ellen. "Have you heard that Mr. Car—that Gino was murdered?" I used his first name to make her feel as if she was speaking to a peer. It seemed like something the good cop in a good cop/bad cop scene might do.

The blush that had covered Mary Ellen's face disappeared, and she went ghostly white. "He—he was—" She mouthed the final word then covered her face with her hands. Apparently she hadn't known.

When she removed her hands, tears were spilling down her cheeks. I felt bad. I could have found a more delicate way to break it to her if I'd realized she hadn't heard yet.

"I'm so sorry to be the one to tell you," I said quite sincerely.

"No, no. No." She turned slightly away from me as she tried to gather herself. "No. No, not at all. Don't feel bad, Fran. I'm glad you told me." She had regained her voice, but tears were still pouring down her cheeks. "What happened?"

"He was poisoned," I said reluctantly. Playing detective had suddenly lost some of its allure.

Mary Ellen gasped. "Oh, good heavens!"

I saw Matt poke his head around a display of earrings then disappear again when he saw Mary Ellen's tears.

"Mary Ellen, since you were a friend of his, I was wondering if you might know of anyone who had a grudge against him, someone who might have wanted to—to hurt him."

She choked back a sob. "No, not a soul. Gino was such a kind man. I-I know he could be abrasive and he rubbed some people the wrong way, but his heart was good. I can't imagine anyone wanting to harm him."

I nodded agreeably and waited until Mary Ellen seemed a bit calmer to ask my next question. "You mentioned you were seeing someone else? What was his name, if you don't mind my asking?"

"His name?" she repeated. Then I saw understanding dawn on her face. "Oh, you don't think Karl—!" She seemed to visibly crumple.

I reached across the counter and rested my hand on hers. She grasped onto it and held it tight.

"Mary Ellen, I'm sorry to even suggest such a thing, and it's not that I even think he may have done it. It's just—Matt's been my friend my whole life, and I'm doing everything I can to give him peace about what happened to his father. I'm trying to talk to everyone I can to see if they can give us any idea who would have done this. If I could just talk to this—this Karl, you said his name was? Since he knew Gino, even though he didn't like him, maybe he could give us a little more insight into his life. I guess Gino wanted to protect Matt from the news that he was dating, so we're discovering this whole other part of his life Matt knew nothing about. We just want to understand him better." I hoped Mary Ellen wouldn't pick up on my somewhat fuzzy, meandering logic.

Mary Ellen straightened her spine and cleared her throat. "His name is Karl Richards. Karl with a K. He's fairly new in town. He works at Paul Hamilton's electrical shop."

"Thank you," I said, squeezing her hand quickly before letting go.

She sniffled, pulled a tissue from underneath the counter, and dabbed at her nose and eyes with it. "I just can't believe someone would do something like that to Gino." She looked past me and out into the store. "Matt? Are you still here?"

Matt appeared from behind some postcards. "Yep, still here." He came toward the counter.

"Matt, Fran here just told me that your father—" She fought back a sob. "That your father was murdered. You can't believe how sorry I am. Gino was just such a wonderful man, and he loved you so much. He talked about you all the time and the important work you did. Fran said that you didn't know he was dating. I'm sure that was just because he didn't want you to think he was trying to replace your mother. I never knew her—I moved to town after she'd passed— but I understand that she was lovely, and I know your father still loved her very much. We would often talk about our late spouses and how different our lives had been since their passing. You know, you're what kept your father going all those years. He loved you more than anything."

Matt was speechless. I didn't think Mr. Cardosi had ever been openly affectionate with Matt, and that was likely the first time he'd ever heard such an enthusiastic expression of his father's love for him.

I saw Matt's Adam's apple bob as he swallowed hard.

"Thank you–" He stopped to clear his throat. "Thank you, uh, Mary Ellen. That means a lot." He raised his hand to his face, probably to wipe away a tear.

I rubbed his shoulder, and he gave me a weak smile of appreciation.

"Do you want to go?" I asked softly. I wasn't sure if Matt would cry in front of me, but I was certain he didn't want to do it in front of Mary Ellen. If we got outside, it would be easier for him to brush it off as the wind blowing something into his eye.

"Yeah," he said quickly.

I turned back to Mary Ellen. "Thank you for your help, Mary Ellen. I know Matt and I both appreciate it."

"Of course, dears. Come back any time. And Matt? If you ever want to talk about your father with someone who cared for him also, please feel free to come by or call me." She handed him a business card with her cell phone number on the bottom. "I also text, if you prefer that. It's something

I was trying to teach your father to do, but Gino was rather set in his ways."

"Yeah, he was," Matt said with a chuckle as he put the business card in his wallet. "And thank you again."

We left the shop and walked slowly toward the beach. I didn't say anything, leaving Matt with his thoughts of his father for the moment. We sat on a bench facing the water. I inhaled the salt air, enjoying the feeling of the breeze trying to pull my hair out of its loose chignon.

"So do you think this other guy Mary Ellen was seeing may have killed my dad?" Matt asked after a while.

"I don't know, but I want to talk to him. She said he works for Paul Hamilton, so I may have to go by there, at least to see what he looks like."

Matt nodded but didn't say anything. His elbows rested on his knees, hands folded, as he stared at the ocean.

"You okay?" I asked.

He nodded again. "Yeah, just hearing Mary Ellen say all that about how much my dad loved me and my mom—you know, that was stuff he never said to me. He wasn't affectionate like that. I guess he thought he had to be a manly man for me. I could have used that growing up—hearing he loved me. I was never sure if he really loved me or just tolerated having me around."

I didn't really know what to say. My mother and grandparents had always been warm and affectionate, giving lots of hugs and kisses and "I love you"s. But I was a girl. Maybe that was the difference. I rubbed his forearm, and he reached across with his other hand and squeezed mine. We stared at the crashing waves, each of us lost in our thoughts.

Chapter Fourteen

I didn't pursue the investigation much more that weekend. I needed to think about how I was going to handle the next step. Since this Karl Richards fellow was new in town, I couldn't rely on my prior knowledge as I had with Mary Ellen. I'd have to do some genuine sleuthing this time. I knew where he worked, but the store was closed on the weekends, so I couldn't go over and poke around until Monday. Monday was when I would see Sammy again and could bring up Karl without seeming overly curious. Matt was the only one who knew I was investigating his father's death, and it seemed best that I keep it that way, at least for the time being. So I lay low.

Matt and I went back to our respective houses after we left the beach on Saturday. Finding the owner of the phone number his dad had been calling had been our only purpose for getting together. It wasn't as if we were dating or doing anything that required spending much time together. And I was absolutely not going to let him pay for a third meal in a row, so not eating together was an easy way to avoid that debate. I spent the rest of Saturday and most of the day Sunday going through my grandparents' things in an effort to start my revamp of the house.

I started in their bedroom partly because that was the room I wanted to move into and partly because they'd been gone long enough that I didn't think it would be as painful to sort out their belongings as it would be my mother's. It was one thing to go into her room to borrow a shirt or some shoes, but to decide which items to throw out or donate to charity? That seemed nearly impossible. Her room still smelled like her. Most of her life had been spent sleeping in that bed and spraying her perfume between those walls. There was even still a stain on the carpet from where she'd spilled nail polish as a teenager. I had every intention of going through her room eventually, but for now, it seemed unbearable.

I started out with the plan to keep one box each of my grandmother's and grandfather's possessions, but as soon as I ran into joint belongings, like the sampler my grandmother had stitched with their names and wedding date, I decided on three boxes—one for her, one for him, and one for them together. Then I made a separate box for items I might want to use to decorate. I'd already decided that I'd never want to or be able to stop feeling their presence and that of my mother in the house, so I wanted to fill a whole wall in the living room with mementos—pictures, samplers, shelves with some particular favorite trinkets. My four-box system resulted in me keeping a bit more than I had planned, but my Donate and Trash piles were substantial enough that I didn't judge myself too harshly.

Monday rolled around, and I headed into the café for my shift, reminding myself that I needed to find a way to casually bring Karl Richards up to Sammy before she left. I needed to do it in a way that didn't seem too suspicious. It was a gorgeous day, sunny and not too hot, so the café wasn't very busy. During the summer, rainy days mid- to late-week were the ones that got us really busy. By then, each week's tourists had gotten comfortable enough with the town to know where they could go to escape the weather and their families at the same time.

"Hey! How was your weekend?" Sammy asked brightly as I came in.

"Pretty good, and yours?"

"It was good. My sister was in town with her kids, so I mostly hung out with them. Compared to where they live, this is the big city, so they had a pretty good time just wandering around town."

"I bet!" I laughed. Sammy's sister lived in the back woods of Maine with her lumber-jack husband and their two kids. I couldn't imagine being that far away and out of touch with civilization.

Sammy and I worked for the next hour or so. I kept on the lookout for opportunities to ask her about Karl Richards, but we were both working pretty steadily, and I didn't get the chance until she was almost ready to leave. The café was quiet. No one was waiting for a drink, all the dishes had been washed, and all the counters were wiped down. Sammy was in the backroom folding some dish rags, so I walked in the back and helped her fold.

"Hey, do you know a guy named Karl Richards?" I asked, trying to sound as casual as I could. "I think he's new in town? I was talking to Mary Ellen over at the souvenir shop the other day, and she mentioned she was dating him. She said he comes in here sometimes, but I couldn't place him, so I thought I'd ask you." A little white lie surely couldn't hurt.

"Karl Richards," she repeated thoughtfully. "I think he works at the electronics shop, doesn't he?"

"Yeah, Mary Ellen mentioned something about that."

"I think he's been in here once or twice. Older guy, kind of nice-looking actually. He looks like he'd be the distinguished older agent in some spy thriller or something. That's about all I know about him. He doesn't say too much, kind of keeps to himself. That's probably why I think he looks like a spy." She giggled as she said it.

I folded some more towels. Quiet and nice-looking wasn't much to go on.

"Oh!" Sammy said after a minute. "He plays chess in the park a lot! I've seen him there on my way home from work."

That was something I could work with. My chess skills were rusty, but I'd be able to talk to him longer and get a better feel for the man from across the chess table than by trying to chat him up at work.

Sammy and I finished folding the towels, and she headed out for the day. The café stayed medium busy the rest of the day, enough so that I stayed on the move but didn't feel frantic or fall behind on keeping things neat. As I walked home that night after closing up, I noticed that it was already getting dark. It always seems unfair that the summer solstice is in June, when the summer months are only just starting. By the end of the summer, it would be dark out long before I closed the café for the night.

That night, as I continued going through my grandparents' things—there was a lot stuffed in that little bedroom!—I came up with my plan for how I would talk to Karl. In the back of my grandfather's closet was an old radio that hadn't worked for as long as

I could remember. In the morning, I'd take that over to the electronics shop and talk to them about getting it fixed. Hopefully I'd run into Karl there and get a look at him. Then, later on, I'd just happen to run into him at the park and try to get myself into a game of chess with him. That would give me plenty of time to get him talking and ever-so-casually bring up Mr. Cardosi. With any luck, he'd slip up and give me some information I could use. It wasn't a foolproof plan—lots of hoping and trying and lucking into things—but it seemed as though it had a decent chance of working. I put the radio by the front door, set my alarm for earlier than I would have liked, and went to bed.

The next morning, bright and early, I headed over to the electronics shop, ancient radio in hand. The door announced my presence with the customary jingle, but no one came out to greet me. I walked in and rested my grandfather's radio on the counter while I waited. After a couple of minutes with no sign of life from the back, I leaned across the counter and looked around. I saw a bell tucked behind the register where it was virtually impossible for a customer to find it. I pulled it around toward me and tapped it rapidly three times.

From the back, I heard old men's voices, but I couldn't make out what they were saying. I could tell there were two of them though. I was getting ready to tap the bell again when an older man came out of the back. He had a thick shock of white hair carefully combed back, and he was wearing a neat black shirt tucked into his khaki pants. I noticed with pleasure that he was wearing a name tag with "Karl" printed on it. Sammy was right—he was pretty nice-looking for an older guy.

"Can I help you?" he asked. He didn't sound as though he particularly wanted to help me, but he didn't sound quite hostile about it either. It was the most neutral, perfunctory tone I could imagine. Certainly not the warm, inviting style of greeting my grandfather had drilled into me.

I smiled my biggest, friendliest smile. "Hi, um, Karl, is it?" I pretended I was just now reading his name tag. I thought I saw him give a brief nod, but it was clear that was all I would get. "I'm Francesca Amaro. I run Antonia's Italian Café down the way." I stuck out my hand.

He took it reluctantly and gave it one hesitant shake before letting go.

"Karl, my late grandfather—" I paused for effect, hoping my grandfather wouldn't mind too much my invoking his memory this way. "Had this old radio in the back of his closet. For the life of me, I can't get it to work, but I have such fond memories of listening to Red Sox games on it with him that I'd love to get it working again. Do you think you can help me?" I was banking on Karl not having relocated to Cape Bay from New York or some other rival baseball team's territory. The one sentence he had uttered didn't sound particularly "Noo Yawk-y," so I thought I was safe.

He pulled the radio toward him and popped open the empty battery compartment. After closing it back up, he plugged the cord in under the counter. He punched a few buttons. As expected, nothing happened.

"We'll take a look." He scrawled out a ticket and handed it to me. He scribbled some more on another piece of paper and taped it onto the radio. He picked it up and turned to walk into the back.

Was that how they treated their customers?

"How much will it be?" I asked.

"Won't know until we figure out what's wrong," he said.

"Well, how will you contact me to let me know?"

"You said you work at Antonia's, right?"

"I own it, yes."

"We'll call you there," he said, not unkindly but not exactly warmly either.

I opened my mouth to say something else, but I couldn't quite figure out what that should be. "Well, thank you!" I gave him a big smile. If he couldn't be polite, at least I could be. "I'll look forward to hearing from you!"

He nodded and disappeared into the back. Mary Ellen certainly had unusual taste in men. For such an exuberant woman, she seemed to like her men quiet and a little grumpy.

There was nothing else I could do there, so I took myself for a walk. Sammy had said that she often saw Karl playing chess at the park in the early afternoons. I wasn't sure what time he usually got there, but I guessed it might be after lunch, when I was supposed to be working. I pulled out my cell phone and called the café. Sammy answered on the second ring.

"Antonia's Italian Café, this is Samantha. How may I help you?" she singsonged.

"Hey, Sammy, it's Fran."

"Oh hey!" she said, much less formally. "What's up?"

"Do you think you could get somebody to cover for me if I took today off?"

Sammy only paused for a second. "Yeah, I'll call Rhonda and see if she can come in."

Rhonda was a little older than me, and she worked for us a few hours a week, mostly during the school year when her kids were out of the house. They were old enough now that she didn't have to be home with them all the time, but she still liked to keep an eye on them when she could.

"Okay, that's great," I said. "Tell her I'll put a little extra in her paycheck for the short notice."

"Oh, you know that'll get her in!" Sammy laughed.

I knew it would. Rhonda mainly worked to fund her occasional trips to Neiman Marcus. A couple hours' work at the café didn't go very far there, but I think she liked being able to buy something from the makeup counter and walk out with a Neiman Marcus bag for everyone to see.

I thanked Sammy and hung up, leaving myself a few hours to wander around town. It was actually fun. Thinking about that furry friend I wanted to get, I walked to the animal shelter across from the police station. I thought about popping in to see if Mike had made any progress on Mr. Cardosi's case, but I figured he didn't need to be bothered, and I didn't have any solid leads of my own yet that I wanted to share.

I walked into the animal shelter and smiled at the girl behind the desk.

"Hello!" I said. "I was wondering if you had any adoptable pets I could look at?"

"Of course!" she replied. "Are you looking for a dog or a cat?"

"I'm not sure yet." I shrugged. "I like both. It just depends on who I fall in love with."

"Not a problem. Everyone's through there," she said, gesturing to a door behind her. "Dogs are on the right, and cats are on the left. Let me know if you have any questions about any of the animals or if you find someone you want to adopt!" She was an exceptionally chipper young woman.

I went into the cat room first. It was much nicer than I remembered. About five kitties shared two large spaces with scratching posts and places to climb and even a few toys. I stopped at each enclosure. They were adorable, but none of them really called out to me.

I went over to the dog space next. It was also much fancier than it had been. That was actually nice to see. I always felt bad for dogs locked in cages that seemed both sterile and filthy at the same time. If the dogs had still been kept that way, I might have adopted them all just out of pity. They all seemed comfortable and happy, but none of them quite made me feel like they were My Dog.

I walked back out into the lobby.

"Find anybody you liked?" she asked.

"No, not today," I said, shaking my head. "But I'll be back."

"That's great!" she replied. "We'll look forward to seeing you!"

I walked outside. I was near the park, so I walked in that direction. I could see the chess tables from the road, so I would be able to see if Karl was there without seeming as though I was spying or lurking.

Only two men were sitting at the tables, and neither one was Karl. I would have to wait to see if he'd show up later.

It was still on the early side, so I ate beach food and strolled around some streets I hadn't been on since my return. I went past my old best friend's house—her family had moved to California when we were in high school. We'd exchanged letters then emails on and off ever since. The new owners had repainted the house and completely changed the front garden, so I had to look at the house number to make sure I was looking at the right place. It reminded me that I should email her—I hadn't told her about my mother's death yet, let alone Mr. Cardosi's. She had also played with Matt when we were kids, and she still asked about him every once in a while.

When I felt as though I'd wandered around long enough that Karl might be at the park, I turned back in that direction. I was on the back side of the park, so I had to go around the pond and up the hill stairs to get to the chess tables. The stairs were at an angle, so I couldn't see anything at the top of them until I came up over the hill. As I crested the hill and came around the

corner, I smiled. Karl was sitting at one of
the chess tables, all by himself.

Chapter Fifteen

I strolled up to him as casually as I could, trying to look as though I was just wandering through the park before I came across my new acquaintance.

"Karl?" I said as I got close.

He looked at me. I could tell he couldn't quite place me at first, but after a few seconds, I saw recognition dawn on his face.

"Francesca. You brought in your grand-father's radio." He still had that very neutral tone.

"Do you mind if I join you?" I asked, smiling and slipping into the seat across from him without waiting for an answer. He had the chess pieces already laid out. "My grandfather used to bring me here to play chess with his buddies when I was a kid. It's been a long time, but I think I can still hold my own if you want to play a game."

He didn't say anything, just nodded and moved his pawn.

We were mostly quiet during the game. That had been my grandfather's style of play also. Whenever I started to be too much of a chatterbox, he would stop playing and lean back with his arms crossed until I noticed and stopped talking. It had taken a while, but I eventually learned my lesson.

I kept up with Karl pretty well for a while, but it was quickly evident that he was a much better player and much more practiced. I managed to work my way out of a check once, but only a couple of moves after that, he called checkmate. I stared at the board in complete surprise. I thought I'd at least had it under control–the checkmate took me completely off guard. I looked at him with my mouth open. I was surprised to see a bit of a smile on his face, the first hint of emotion I had seen from him. He reached his hand across the table for me to shake.

"I didn't even see that coming," I said as we shook hands.

"I think your grandfather would be proud if that's how you play when you've been away from the game for a while. I thought I had you a couple times, but you made good moves to get out of it."

"Thank you," I said. That really felt like a genuine compliment. "So you're new in town, right?"

He seemed to give me a suspicious look as we went about setting the pieces back up. "I am."

"What brought you to Cape Bay?" I felt as though he wasn't eager to answer the question, so I kept talking in an effort to set him at ease. "Friends? Family? Just looking to retire by the sea?"

He continued eyeing me, but at least he answered. "Retirement. The beach seemed like a good place to start this part of my life."

"Well, that's nice!" I said cheerily, trying to keep the conversation going. "Do you have any grandkids that'll be coming to visit you? I can imagine Grandpa living by the beach would be quite a draw!"

"No kids, no grandkids," he said briefly.

"Oh well, at least you don't have to worry about them tracking sand all over your house then!" I was trying to keep the conversation going even though I felt as if I was sinking. "How long have you been in town?"

"Few months."

"Oh, just in time for the summer tourist season! Well, after Labor Day, things will calm down quite a bit. We get tourists all year 'round, but summer is naturally the busiest." I glanced at him. He didn't have much of a reaction, so I kept going. "This summer has been especially crazy for me. I grew up here, but I was living in New York until a couple of months ago. My mom—I don't know if you got to meet her—her name was Carmella? She ran Antonia's?"

He didn't really give any indication as to whether he had met her or not.

I went on. "She passed away a couple months ago, and I moved back to run the café. Then just a few weeks ago, my neighbor Gino Cardosi—he was the town barber?—*he* died." Still no reaction. I decided to go for broke. I leaned in. "And there's a rumor that he was *murdered*. Can you believe it? A murder in Cape Bay? It's been a crazy summer!"

I leaned back and watched his face. I saw something flicker across it, but I wasn't sure what it was. What was clear was that he was frowning more than he had been, and he was picking up the chess pieces instead of putting them down.

"I didn't realize the time. I have to go," he said brusquely and without looking at his watch. He put the pieces all back into their spaces in the case and closed it. "Nice playing with you."

He walked away before I had a chance to fully process what was going on. I had obviously hit a nerve with my comments about Mr. Cardosi. I sat at the table, completely stunned. Who acted like that? And how guilty did it make him look? Very guilty, in my opinion.

I looked around to see if any of the other chess players had noticed Karl's peculiar behavior. It didn't seem that anyone had. They were all going about their games, oblivious to what had just happened at my table. I stood slowly and walked through the park, still baffled by the turn of events.

Confused as I was, I knew I wanted to go home and get online to see what I could find out about Karl Richards.

I walked quickly through the park, down the stairs, and around the pond. I arrived back at my house and headed straight up the stairs to my room to get my laptop. As usual, it took forever to boot up, but once it did, Karl spelling his name with a K instantly made my investigation easier.

Six months ago, Karl Richards, age 61, had been released from prison after completing a twenty-year sentence for multiple counts of robbery.

I leaned back in my chair and stared at the computer. There was no way that was right. But right there in front of my disbelieving eyes was his mug shot. He was younger in the picture, with fewer lines on his face and much darker hair, but his hair was just as thick and still combed back in the same style. Besides, the caption laid it out for me:

Karl Richards, now age 61, as he looked upon his sentencing

I read the accompanying article that had been published after his release. Conveniently for me, it gave a detailed overview of his case for people who didn't know about or remember his crimes. Apparently Karl had spent years breaking into the homes of the rich residents of Boston, picking their safes, and stealing their highest-priced valuables. Detectives were stuck for over a decade as the robberies continued. The jewels never showed up in local pawn shops or at any traceable auctions, foreign or domestic, despite the astronomically high prices they would bring. The police came to the conclusion that they had been sold directly to overseas buyers who had the wisdom not to resell them. But the robberies continued. No matter how sophisticated a security system someone installed, Karl, or the Filigree Filcher as the media took to calling him before they knew his identity, managed to get past it.

Homeowners and the police tried everything from stakeouts to booby traps. The Filigree Filcher didn't seem to have any kind of pattern, rhyme, or reason to his thefts. The police couldn't determine any connection between the victims beyond their wealth and exquisite taste in jewelry. He'd go quiet for so long that everyone assumed that he must have died, moved away, or been arrested for an unrelated crime. Then he'd pop back up, stealing something more glamorous and expensive than anything he'd stolen before and from a house with an even more elaborate security system.

It wasn't until a good fifteen years into his thievery that a homeowner managed to rig up a night vision camera system that got a picture of the Filigree Filcher in action without him realizing. They plastered his image all over the news and newspapers, and it only took a few days for someone to identify the man in the picture as mild-mannered Karl Richards, who worked as an electrical engineer for a popular stereo maker.

When the police searched his home, they were shocked to find every single piece of jewelry that had been stolen over the years packed into shoe boxes and tucked away into his closet. He hadn't sold, given away, or otherwise divested himself of anything he had taken. The mountain of evidence against him was insurmountable. Despite that, he refused to plead guilty and was convicted of every last charge at trial. He declined to ever give a reason for his crimes. Because of the sheer number of thefts and the hundreds of millions of dollars the jewelry added up to, he was sentenced to twenty years in prison. He'd had opportunities to get out on parole, and he had declined all of them. He didn't leave prison until he had served every last day of his sentence.

Even after reading the whole article, and several others I found online, I still couldn't quite believe it. "Retirement" indeed! He'd moved to Cape Bay because he was too well-known to go back to Boston! I wondered if he was still up to his crimes. Not that we had the kind of fabulously wealthy people with extravagant jewelry that Boston had. And I hadn't heard of any robberies. News like that traveled fast in our small town. Whether or not that was what he was up to, though, what I knew was that I was looking at a known criminal who had a clear motive to murder Mr. Cardosi—they were both dating the same woman. *And* they'd openly despised each other.

Then I thought of something else. What if Mr. Cardosi had done the same Internet search I had? He hadn't been a very techno-logically savvy guy, but I'd seen a computer in his house and it wasn't really that hard to do a search. That lent a whole new element of intrigue to the case. If Mr. Cardosi had known about Karl's criminal history and threatened to tell Mary Ellen about it if Karl didn't back off, then Karl would have not one but two motives for murder.

For the first time since I'd started looking into Mr. Cardosi's death, I had a murder suspect.

Chapter Sixteen

My mind was swirling with my discovery. I wondered if the police knew, if they'd gotten this far in their investigation. I debated calling Mike right away to share what I'd learned, but I decided I should fill Matt in first. He was at work, of course, and this wasn't the kind of information I could give by text or over the phone, so I'd have to wait until he got home. I grabbed my cell phone to send him a text.

I found out something kind of big. Can we get together tonight?

I went back to my computer and looked at Karl's mug shot again. Murder was a far cry from robbery, but I imagined that twenty years in prison could change a man. Still, was that the face of a man who would kill another man? Could the man who had complimented my chess game have murdered my neighbor? That was where the evidence was pointing, and a good investigator couldn't ignore the evidence.

My text message alert sounded. I went back over and picked up my phone.

Sure. Want to get dinner too?

Dinner sounded good, but only if I was paying. I texted him back to say so. His reply came in quickly.

Yeah, we'll see about that. ;)

A winky face! What did a winky face mean? Was it just a casual, joking reference to our ongoing debate on who was paying, or was he flirting with me? I wasn't sure and I didn't necessarily think it required a reply, so I left it alone.

I picked up the little notebook I'd been keeping my notes in. It was almost full. I needed to buy another one, but for now, I'd just go back to my legal pad. I flipped through the pages until I got to a blank one. There, I wrote down every detail of my two interactions with Karl Richards and a summary of what I'd found online, complete with the URLs of the articles I'd consulted.

By the time I was done, it was late afternoon, so I didn't have long to wait before Matt got off work. I went downstairs and worked through some more of my grandparents' things. I was making good progress. I'd completely finished both of their closets when I heard my text message alert. I was concerned that Matt might be cancelling our dinner, and I was surprised to see that it was already past five. I must have gotten way more involved in sorting and categorizing than I'd realized.

Heading your way. Hope you're hungry.

I put a last couple of things in boxes then headed upstairs to check my hair and makeup. It wasn't that I wanted to make sure I looked good for Matt. It had just been a fairly long day, and I was certain that I looked like a mess. But I didn't look as bad as I thought. I tucked a few hairs back in place, touched up my makeup, and decided I was satisfied.

The doorbell conveniently rang at that moment. I ran downstairs, checked the peephole to make sure it was Matt, and pulled the door open. He was grinning and holding a pizza.

"Hungry?" he asked as he stepped past me.

I just stood there gawking at him and the food that he'd paid for. "You sneak!" I fully realized that was such a weak insult it didn't even deserve to be called one.

"I thought it would be easier if we just ate in," he called over his shoulder as he walked toward the kitchen.

"But I was supposed to pay for dinner tonight!" I shut the door and followed him.

"Oh yeah!" he said innocently. "I completely forgot!"

"You lie!"

He shrugged. "Yeah, maybe." He put the pizza on the counter. "What goes with pizza? Red or white? What do you have?"

"I have red," I said, stalking across the kitchen to the wine rack.

I pulled out a bottle I thought would go well with pizza and slapped it into his hand. I pulled open the drawer where I kept the corkscrew and handed it to him. Matt opened the bottle as I got two glasses.

He filled them generously and handed me one. I wasn't actually mad at him for buying dinner yet again, but I didn't want to take advantage of him.

"I got margherita. I hope that's okay. I figured it was simple and classic enough I couldn't really go wrong."

Margherita was fine by me. As far as I was concerned, simple and classic was the only way to go with pizza. We sat and ate at the kitchen table, sipping our wine between bites.

"So what was it you wanted to tell me?" Matt asked when we were finished.

I took a deep breath and anxiously played with the stem of my wine glass. This was big news, and I wasn't quite sure how to tell him.

"Franny?" he said after I had remained silent for a good minute or two.

"I managed to talk to Karl Richards—that guy who was also dating Mary Ellen. He was kind of weird, especially when I mentioned your dad's murder. He basically just got up and walked away. So I looked him up online."

"And?" Matt prompted when I fell silent again.

I took another deep breath. "And it turns out he's a convicted felon. Robbery, but he spent twenty years in jail. I-I think he might have killed your dad."

Matt looked at me in silence. I couldn't tell what he was thinking. When I noticed the way he was working his jaw, though, I had a pretty good idea.

"You think he killed my dad over Mary Ellen?" he asked after a moment.

"That, and I think it's possible that your dad found out about Karl's criminal record and tried to use it to pressure him to break up with her."

"You have evidence of that?" he asked.

"No," I admitted. "But I think it's something the police need to be aware of. I thought I'd go talk to Mike about it tomorrow."

Matt nodded. "I think that's a good idea. They should look into it as soon as possible. If he killed my dad, I want him in jail, not out walking the streets."

"I'll go first thing in the morning," I assured him. "Do you want to come with me?"

"No, I'll let you handle it. I—" He seemed to be looking for the right words, maybe to say that he wanted to think about the circumstances of his father's death as little as possible. He shook his head slightly. "I'll let you handle it."

We talked for a little while longer, some about his dad and some about other things. I told him about my plan to sort through all of my mother's and grandparents' things and redecorate the house in more my style. He suggested that I work on his dad's house when I was done at mine. He was making a good effort to keep up the conversation, but I could tell his mind was elsewhere. Eventually he admitted it and said he should probably just go home so he could be alone with his thoughts.

"Are you sure you'll be okay?" I asked as I walked him to the door.

"Yeah. I just need to go home and chill out and get some rest."

I eyed him warily. "You're not going to do anything stupid, are you?" Matt had never been the violent type, but he'd never before dealt with the possibility of knowing the identity of the man who had killed his father.

"No! No," Matt scoffed. "That's for the police to handle." He rubbed his face. "I just need to go home and turn on the ball game or something and chill out. No offense." He put a hand on my shoulder.

"None taken. We all need personal time."

He pulled me into a hug. "Thank you for looking into this. I know the police are too, but I know it's personal for you. It makes it a little easier knowing someone who cares so much is on it."

"Of course, Matty," I said. "You know I'll do anything I can to help get this all wrapped up for you. You shouldn't have to deal with your father's murder being unsolved for one second longer than you have to."

"Thank you." He rubbed his hands up and down my back. He finally let me go and headed out to his car.

I went straight upstairs to review my notes again before bed. I had a big day coming up, and I wanted make sure I was ready.

I woke up excited and raring to go. I wanted to look professional, like someone whose opinion a police officer would take seriously, so I pulled out one of the outfits I used to wear to make presentations to clients in New York and put that on. I styled my hair a little more than I'd been doing to go to work at the café. All in all, I thought it came together nicely. I got my notes together and made sure they were in order so I could refer to them quickly if Mike had any questions. I gave myself one last glance in the mirror and headed for the police station.

"Is Mike Stanton in?" I asked the woman at the front desk.

She looked at me over her glasses. "Who can I tell him is here?"

I gave her a big, professional smile. "Francesca Amaro."

She looked at me again then pulled off her glasses. "Fran? It's me, Margaret. Margaret Robbins. From high school."

I stared at her. The name sounded familiar, but the face didn't register.

"Cheerleading squad?" she prompted.

All of a sudden, it clicked. I could see her in my mind's eye in a short cheerleading skirt with her long hair pulled up into a high ponytail. "Margaret! I'm so sorry! I've just been running into so many people I haven't seen in years, and it's taking a while to place everyone."

"Oh no, I understand. I didn't recognize you until you said your name." She paused. "I'm very sorry about your mother. And you found Gino Cardosi's body, didn't you? Is that what you're here to talk to Mike about? Let me call him for you." She picked up her desk phone and punched a few buttons.

I remembered something else about her as she murmured into the phone—it had always been hard to get a word in edgewise when talking to her.

She hung up and smiled at me. "If you want to have a seat over there, Mike will be out in just a minute."

I thanked her and sat in one of the ancient pleather chairs lining the walls of the lobby. I took a deep breath. I was actually getting a little nervous. I felt good about my theory—it was solid—but I wasn't sure how Mike would feel about me doing my own investigating. I didn't want him to feel as though I was invading his turf, but I'd felt strongly that I needed to help Matt. I had a duty to him as his friend and to his father as the one who found his body.

Mike stepped into the lobby and glanced around the room for me. He gave me a tight smile when he saw me. "Fran? If you'd like to come with me?"

He held open the door that he had just come through. I felt unnervingly as though he were calling me back to be questioned instead of me coming to give him information. I walked through the door, and he led me to a small, windowless room that I suspected they used for interrogations. It didn't lessen the weird feeling I had in the pit of my stomach.

"Have a seat," Mike said, gesturing at the lone metal chair in the room.

I sat and put my notes on the table. I noticed that my hands were shaking. I'd never been in the interrogation room of a police station before. The atmosphere must be getting to me.

Mike perched on the edge of the table. "So what can I help you with today, Fran?"

This was a different Mike from the one I'd seen in the initial stages of the investigation. That Mike had been warm and jovial, the guy I grew up with. This Mike was stern and terse. I had a feeling that if this were a good cop/bad cop situation, I would be dealing with the bad cop. I had to look up to talk to him and couldn't help but wonder if that was an intentional power move, like when a talk show host's chair is ever-so-subtly raised six inches above his guests. Even though I was there of my own volition, it all made me nervous.

I inhaled deeply and spread my hands on the table to steady them. "Well, Mike, I'm here because—" I took another deep breath and looked him dead in the eye. "I'm here because I know who killed Gino Cardosi."

Chapter Seventeen

Mike raised his eyebrows and was silent for a moment longer than I was comfortable with. "You know who killed Gino Cardosi," he finally said slowly.

I nodded. "Yes, I do."

Mike looked at me silently for longer than I would have liked. "And who is that?"

"Karl Richards. You might not know him. He's new in town, but I did some investigating, and I'm confident that he did it."

"You are," Mike said, more as a statement than a question. The way he kept using that flat tone of voice was making me nervous.

"Yes." I flipped through a couple of pages of my notes, looking for the one that had my findings about Karl. "See, he and Mr. Cardosi were both dating Mary Ellen Chapman, which in and of itself isn't necessarily a huge motive for murder, but I did some research online..." I hesitated when Mike stood and started walking back and forth on the other side of the room, his arms crossed. I wasn't sure what that was about, so I just kept going. "And I found out that he has a criminal record. A major one. Six months ago—"

Mike spun around and slammed his hands on the table. "Do you think I don't know that?" He sounded really pretty angry.

"Um, I don't—I didn't think—"

"You didn't think what?"

"I didn't think you knew the thing about Mary Ellen. I only found out because Matt and I went looking for Mr. Cardosi's cell phone because Chris at the cell phone shop told me Mr. Cardosi was looking for a new one, and when Matt and I found it, there were just a bunch of calls to Mary Ellen's number—" I was rambling, but Mike was making me nervous.

"Have you ever heard of phone records, Fran?" Mike asked, sounding exasperated.

"Yes." Of course I had. That was what the phone company sent me every month with my cell phone bill—a complete record of everyone I'd called. *Oh.*

"We're the police. The first thing we do when we have a murder victim is pull his phone records. We don't have to go looking for his cell phone. The phone company knows all that. Hell, the phone company can give us the contents of all his text messages. Sent *and* received."

I was starting to feel a little bad. As soon as Mike said it, it made perfect sense that they had pulled Mr. Cardosi's phone records and knew everyone he'd talked to. But the thing about Karl Richards—that had to be new information, right? Against my better judgement, I said it. "But Karl Richards—?"

He rubbed his face. I got the sense he couldn't believe he was having this conversation.

"Karl Richards just finished serving twenty years in prison. You think he's going to kill somebody so he can get himself sent right back?"

"You think he's not?" I asked, a little indignant. He couldn't just blow off my theory because he thought Karl would abide by the law so he could avoid prison. Prison hadn't seemed to scare him very much over the fifteen years he was stealing jewelry and hoarding the evidence. "You don't think Mr. Cardosi could have found out about Karl's criminal record and threatened to out him to Mary Ellen? You don't think Karl could have killed him to stop him?"

"No, I don't," Mike said firmly.

"And why not?" I asked.

"Because he was at his doctor's office in Boston when Gino Cardosi was killed."

Oh. Well, that changed things. I went from feeling a little bad to a lot bad. And like maybe my detective skills weren't as good as I thought they were. The metal chair I was sitting in suddenly felt very cold and hard. I tried to think of where I had gone wrong, what lead I'd failed to track down. Apparently I'd forgotten to check Karl's alibi, but it had seemed like such a slam dunk!

"You can't go poking your nose in police business," Mike said, interrupting my thoughts. "There's a reason why we don't just leave it to civilians to solve crimes. Hell, there's a reason we don't just let rookies investigate crimes on their own! It's hard. It takes training. A lot can go wrong, and you can ruin someone's life by accusing them of a crime. It's not something to be taken lightly!"

I couldn't remember ever seeing Mike so worked up, except maybe on the football field in high school. It made me realize why police interrogations worked so well. Normal Mike was a pleasant enough guy, but this version of him was a little scary. If I'd committed a crime, I'd be shaking in my boots from watching him pace around and rant and rave.

He took a deep breath, as if he was trying to calm himself down. "Look, I know you were just trying to help Matt figure out what happened to his dad, but you can't just go messing in people's lives. Do you know how freaked out Karl was after you talked to him? He thought you were going to tell the whole town that he was a convicted jewel thief. He thought he would have to pick up and move again to get away from the rumors. He's an old man, Fran, and he's paid his debt to society. It's not up to you to make him continue paying."

I barely heard the rest of what Mike said after he mentioned that Karl had been freaked out after I'd talked to him. *How did he know that?* I held up my hand to stop him. "How did you know I talked to Karl?"

Mike sighed. "He came in here and told me."

I was confused. "He just walked in here and told you that? Why?"

"Like I said, because he was worried."

"So he just came in here and confessed that he was a jewel thief and said he was worried that I was going to drive him out of town?"

Mike looked at me as if I wasn't getting something obvious. "I'd already questioned him, Francesca."

He'd used my full name. That was bad.

"When I identified him as a suspect, I pulled his criminal record," Mike said. "I interviewed him and asked him about it. Then when you showed up, talking to him about the Cardosi case, he got worried and came in to talk to me. He moved here to start a new life where people didn't know his name and his face, and you took that from him. You think something like that will stay a secret for long in Cape Bay? And what do you think Mary Ellen'll do when she finds out? You think she'll just be cool with it? God, Fran, you've got to just leave it alone from here on out, okay? No more investigating, no more slinking around asking people questions. You've got to cool it, okay?"

I nodded. I was embarrassed to say the least. I thought I'd been slick enough that Karl hadn't realized I suspected him of anything, but apparently I was wrong. I'd accidentally tipped him off to my sleuthing, which wasn't exactly a brilliant investigative technique, and possibly ruined his newfound anonymity and romantic relationship. I hadn't set out to ruin anybody's life—at least, no one other than the person who'd killed Mr. Cardosi—but apparently I'd done that, or nearly done it anyway. "I'm sorry, Mike."

"I'm not the one you owe an apology," he said curtly.

I nodded. I did owe Karl an apology. I might not be able to fix what I'd done, but I could at least let him know I was sorry.

Mike stood there for another minute or so before he asked me if there was anything else I wanted to share with him.

"No," I said quietly. "There's nothing else."

"Do you need a minute, or are you ready to go?"

Apparently I was more visibly shaken up than I realized. "I'm ready to go." I gathered up my papers.

Mike put his hand on the doorknob then looked back at me. "Just so you know, I'm not mad at you. Like I said, I know you were just trying to help Matt, and I know it's personal for you because you found the body. And that's on top of you already having a rough summer. Just try to chill out a little, okay?"

I nodded as I picked up my notes and walked to the door. Mike patted my back as we went out.

"I'll see you around," he said as he bid me good-bye in the lobby.

"See you," I replied.

I walked outside and stood on the sidewalk, facing the park. I could go straight across the park toward home, where I could crawl back into bed or curl up on the couch to watch some crappy daytime TV court shows. Or I could turn left and go to the café to bury myself in work for a while. But I turned right to go down the street to Paul Hamilton's electronics shop. I wanted to apologize.

Chapter Eighteen

After my first visit, I knew not to expect anyone at the electronics shop to appear immediately upon my arrival, but it still took so long that I was hunting for the bell before Karl came out to greet me. He didn't exactly look excited to have a customer in the first place, but his face got even more miserable-looking when he saw me.

"If you're here about your radio, it'll be ready tomorrow," he said by way of greeting.

"That's actually not why I'm here, but thank you." I had butterflies in my stomach.

I always got nervous when I had to admit to screwing up or doing something wrong, but when I had to admit to a man that I had thought he was a murderer and had even gone to the police to tell them, I was extra nervous.

He just stared at me. I guessed if I wasn't there about my grandfather's radio, he wasn't interested in finding out what I did want. Not that I blamed him, under the circumstances. I tried to smile. We were standing barely a couple of feet apart with only the counter between us. I wasn't sure if anyone was in the back, but I thought I heard some shuffling. Assuming that whoever was back there didn't know about Karl's history, I didn't want to negate my apology by filling them in.

"Karl, I understand that I owe you an apology," I said quietly.

He gave no indication that he'd heard me but none that he hadn't either.

"I made some assumptions and leapt to some conclusions and came up with something that was totally wrong. I should have stayed out of it and let the police do their job. I'm sorry," I said.

He stared at me for a few seconds then gave me the slightest of nods. "Thank you." We looked at each other for a few more seconds. "Is there anything else?"

"No," I replied. "That's all."

"We'll call you when your radio's done," he said and turned to go into the back.

He was a strange man for sure, but I didn't fault him for not wanting to hang around talking to me. I waited until he had disappeared, just to make sure he wasn't going to suddenly turn around and come back, then left to go home. I could have gone to work, but I needed to think. I tucked my papers under my arm and shoved my hands in my pockets as I walked toward the park and its shortcut to my house.

It had been, by pretty much every imaginable measure, a pretty awful summer. First my fiancé had left me, then my mother passed away, then Mr. Cardosi was murdered, then I accused an innocent man of the crime. At least only one of those things was my fault. The rest of it was just the universe trying to mess with me. What doesn't kill you makes you stronger, right? That was what my mother would have said anyway. So far the only good that had come out of the past few months was getting to quit my job and escape the New York City rat race. That, and getting to reconnect with Matt. Spending time with Matt again was like getting transported back in time to my high school days, but without all the awkwardness that came with being in high school. Being with him now was just fun. I was my adult self, with all of my knowledge and confidence, but without all the awkwardness that usually came with dating someone new. Not that Matt and I were dating. We just didn't have any getting-to-know-you discomfort when we hung out.

Being so off-balance from all the changes in my personal life had to be how I'd gone so wrong with the whole Karl debacle. Everything I'd relied on for so many years had been completely upended. I'd latched on to my investigation of Mr. Cardosi's murder as something to give me purpose and direction, but work could give me that. Redecorating my house could give me that. My friends—Matt and Sammy—could give me that. My new pet could give me that, as soon as I found him. I didn't need to be an amateur detective to have purpose, especially since I was apparently pretty terrible at it. My work, my house, my friends, and my pet would be my focus. That was what I would do with myself and my time.

I was in the park, walking past the chess tables. A dog ran along by the tree line. It stood out to me because stray dogs weren't common in Cape Bay. I thought he must have gotten off his leash or escaped his yard. He didn't have a collar, but I remembered one time when I was a kid and my best friend and I were walking her dog. He had managed to slip completely out of his collar and left us standing with an empty collar hanging from the leash. I wondered if this dog had done the same thing. He didn't seem particularly interested in or afraid of me. He just ran along, roughly keeping pace with me as I walked fairly quickly through the park. Eventually, though, he turned off and ran down the hill ahead of me, as if he'd suddenly realized he had somewhere to be.

It must not have been too far away, though, because as I got toward the stairs, I heard him barking. The closer I got, the louder and more frantic it got. I usually almost ran down the stairs, but when I reached the top, I realized the dog was right at the bottom, barking furiously. I hesitated, resting my hand on the railing. Just as I decided not to show the strange dog any fear and lifted my foot to take the first step, I felt something sweep my feet out from under me.

I yelped as my face flew down toward the steep concrete stairs. My papers went flying, and I barely stopped myself from tumbling down the stairs head over heels. If my hand hadn't already been on the railing, I wouldn't have been able to stop myself. Sharp pain shot up my right leg as I twisted on it in an attempt to regain my footing. The dog flew up the stairs past me, still barking loudly. My arm wrenched as my body rotated toward the top of the stairs. I saw feet clad in men's shoes disappearing back toward the chess tables, assisted by the cane I instinctively knew had been used to trip me. The dog perched on the top stair, barking at the fleeing feet.

I struggled to my feet to follow the tripper and his cane, but as soon as I put weight on my leg, it gave out beneath me. With the amount of pain I felt, there was no way I was walking anywhere. I wiggled around so that I was sitting on one of the steps, my hurt leg stretched out in front of me. I tensed up when the dog came down the couple of stairs to where I was sitting. When he immediately shoved his wet nose into my palm, I calmed down, though. He was a friendly dog. His mouth was shaped as if he were smiling. Medium-sized with scruffy gray and brown fur, he looked like a stray. I wondered where he had come from.

It occurred to me, if not for his barking, I would have been going a lot faster and not holding onto the stair railing when I was tripped. He wasn't just friendly—he was *my* friend. I scratched his head in thanks.

As soon as I did, as if that indicated to him that I was okay, he ran back up the stairs and barked again. I turned as best I could to look up toward where he was standing, but he disappeared from my view and his barking faded. I sighed. Maybe he wasn't my friend after all. I was glancing around at my notes scattered all over the ground and trying to figure out how I'd get myself up or down the stairs when I heard his barking get louder again. I looked back up to see the dog return. He scampered down the stairs, bumped his nose against me, then took off back up the stairs, barking furiously. The barking got fainter then louder as he repeated his run-away-and-come-back pattern. I wondered if it was possible that he was trying to get help. That seemed like an out-there idea and I hadn't exactly had the best track record with crazy ideas lately, but what else could he be doing, running back and forth like that?

I couldn't just sit there and wait, even if he was trying to help me. I glanced up and down the stairs. I had definitely landed closer to the top than the bottom. I pushed my right heel into one of the steps below me. Pain shot back up my leg. Definitely my knee hurt. I tested my left leg. That one had been spared. I braced my palms against the step above me and pushed up with my arms and my left leg. I only had a few steps to get up. As long as I didn't put any pressure on my right leg, I was okay. I worked my way up the stairs as the dog continued to race back and forth. I crested the stairs and scooted off to the edge of the sidewalk.

The dog raced back again and sat on the pavement next to me. He kept barking, so loud it hurt my ears a little, and I had to lean away. Even so, I couldn't help but reach out to scratch my new buddy's chest.

"Franny, is that you? Are you okay?"

I looked up, shocked to hear Matt's voice. "Yeah, I just had a little tumble."

Matt hurried over and crouched down beside me.

"What are you doing here?" I asked. At that time of day, I expected him to be at work.

"Looking for you. What happened? Did you trip over your feet or something?"

"More like I was tripped."

Matt looked startled. "You were *what*?"

I sighed. "I was walking home from the police station, and someone with a cane tripped me when I got to the stairs. If it wasn't for this guy, I would have gone down a lot harder." I gestured toward the dog.

"Are you hurt?" he asked, looking me up and down and seeming to focus on the awkward way I was holding my leg.

"I twisted my knee. I can't really put weight on it."

"God, Franny, we need to get you to a doctor. Come on, let me help you up."

Matt stood and reached down to help me to my feet. Well, to my foot, since the left one was the only one doing me much good at the moment. He stood on my right side and wrapped his arm around my waist.

"We'll get you out to the street, then I'll run and get my car, okay?" he asked.

"Okay," I replied. We started limping along. "Wait! We need to bring the dog!"

Matt looked back at the mutt still sitting on the ground where I'd been.

"Are you sure he doesn't belong to someone?" he asked me.

"No, but he doesn't have a collar. He saved me. The least we can do is help him find his owner if he has one."

"All right." Matt shrugged. He patted his leg with his free hand. "Come on, boy!"

The dog popped up and trotted over to us, following along as we limped out to the street.

Chapter Nineteen

"Can we drop the dog off at my house?" I asked as Matt pulled his car away from the curb. "He can't stay in the car while we're at the urgent care."

Matt looked skeptical. "Are you sure you want to drop some strange dog off in your house then leave it for a few hours?"

"Well, what do you suggest?" I asked.

"For you to worry more about your leg and less about the dog. How's it doing there? Does it have enough support?"

Matt had put his briefcase and a balled-up sweatshirt under my heel to keep my leg straight and propped up.

"It's okay," I replied. "I'm sure it can wait a while if you think it would be better to run to a store and pick up some food and a crate for him."

"That's not exactly what I meant," Matt said. "You know he probably belongs to someone, right?"

I wanted to think that he didn't actually. He was friendly and comfortable with people, but he was on the thin side, as though he hadn't been getting enough to eat lately.

"Yes," I said reluctantly. "But don't you think they'd want him to be safe and well taken care of until they can be reunited?"

Matt rolled his eyes. "Don't you think they're more likely to look for him at the shelter than in your house?"

As much as I didn't want to admit it, I knew he was right. "I guess so."

"Besides, they'll be able to get him all checked out and dewormed or whatever." Matt pulled the car into the animal shelter's parking lot.

"Okay." I sighed as he got out of the car. "But make sure you give them my name! I want that dog if no one comes for him!"

"Yes, ma'am." Matt opened the back door to let the dog out.

The little mutt obediently followed him into the shelter as if it was the most normal thing in the world and he'd known Matt for years.

"Bye, Latte!" I called softly, waving. I'd already started thinking of the dog as Latte because his fur was the exact shade of a perfectly mixed latte. I really hoped he'd come home with me someday soon.

I wiggled around to get my phone out of my pocket while I waited for Matt to come back out. I had four texts and two missed calls from Matt. I'd completely forgotten that I'd put my phone on silent when I went into the police station. I turned the volume back up and had just opened the Internet browser when Matt came back out of the shelter. A big smile broke across my face when I saw Latte tripping along beside him.

Matt opened the car's rear door and guided Latte in with a new bright-blue leash. Matt tossed a baggie of dog food in behind him.

"What happened?" I asked, trying to restrain my glee as Matt got back in the car.

He sighed. "If someone finds a lost dog, they encourage them to keep it. She said it's better for the dogs. She scanned him for a microchip, which he didn't have, took a picture for their website, and gave me enough food to get him through until we can get to the store. I guess you get to take him home after all."

I clapped and squealed as if I was eight years old. I twisted around as best I could to look at Latte without hurting my leg. "Do you want to come home with me, Latte? Would you like that? I have to go to the doctor for a little bit, but when I come home, we can snuggle on the couch and—"

"Wait, did you already name the dog?" Matt interrupted.

"Well, I couldn't just keep calling him 'the dog'! Especially not if he's coming home with me!"

Matt just shook his head. He drove us over to my house to drop Latte off.

"Put him in the upstairs bathroom—it's bigger than the downstairs one," I said. We'd decided that locking Latte in a bathroom would be the best bet for the time being so he wouldn't get overwhelmed by a big new house and go crazy. "And don't forget to give him a big bowl of food and water. He looks hungry, don't you, Latte?" I scratched his chin one more time before Matt got him out of the car.

When Matt came out, he drove me to the doctor, who said I had definitely sprained my knee and would have to wear a brace for a few weeks until it healed. Elevate, rest, cold compresses, and painkillers.

"Do you have anyone at home to help you out around the house until you're back on your feet?" the doctor asked.

Before I could say I didn't but that I would be fine on my own, Matt interrupted. "I can take care of her."

I looked at him, surprised. "You don't have to do that."

He shrugged. "I don't mind."

We picked up some burgers and fries on the way back to my house—after I'd called Sammy to tell her what had happened, of course. With all the excitement, I'd completely forgotten that I hadn't eaten until suddenly I was starving. I tried to get Matt to let me pay, but he just refused to take my credit card with him when he went inside. I surreptitiously stuffed fries in my mouth as he drove, and Matt pretended he didn't notice.

When we got to the house, Matt got my crutches out of the backseat and helped me navigate my way inside, then he went upstairs to let Latte out of the bathroom. Latte raced down the stairs and ran around the house until he found me in the kitchen. He jumped up and licked my face. I knew I should stop him from putting his paws on the table to reach me, but it was so sweet that he was so excited to see me that I figured I'd let him do it just this once.

When Matt and I finished eating, he helped me into the living room and got my leg propped up with some pillows on the couch. Latte jumped up with me at first, but that was a little uncomfortable, so he ended up lying on the floor beside me. Matt sat in my grandfather's old recliner.

"You know, we should probably call the police if someone deliberately tripped you down the stairs," he said.

"Yeah." I thought for a minute. "Who in town walks with a cane? Or maybe a limp?"

"Other than you?" Matt asked.

"I use crutches, thank you very much."

Matt chuckled. "A lot of people use a cane. Half of this street uses a cane." Matt studied my face. "This is getting dangerous, Franny. Don't you think it's a little suspicious that as soon as you leave the police station after telling the cops about this Karl guy, you get tripped down the stairs?" Realization dawned across Matt's face. "Wait, does Karl walk with a cane?"

I hadn't told Matt yet about my meeting with Mike. He didn't know that Karl was *not* the man who had killed his father.

"Um, no," I said.

"Franny?" I could hear in Matt's voice that he knew I wasn't telling him something.

"Karl's not the one who killed your dad. Mike already talked to him, and he was at the doctor's in Boston during the murder. I don't know who did it, but apparently someone thinks I do, and they're trying to stop me."

Matt stared at me for a minute, then he stood and walked across the room. He pulled his phone out of his pocket and dialed a number.

"Matty? Who are you calling? Matty?"

He didn't answer, but whoever he was calling did. "Hi, it's Matt Cardosi. How're you doing today?... good, good. Look, the reason I'm calling—somebody tripped Franny at the stairs in the park today and she messed up her knee pretty good. I don't know if this is related to what happened to my dad, but we need to file a police report either way... yeah... yeah... okay... yeah... okay, see you in a few minutes... thanks, Mike. Bye." Matt turned around and looked at me. "Franny, I know you feel strongly about finding whoever killed my dad, and obviously I do too, but not at the expense of your life! You could've broken your neck falling down those stairs! Mike'll be here in a few minutes to take a report. Will you just take a step back and let the police handle this?"

"Matty, whoever it was pushed me down the stairs! He may not have been trying to kill me, but he was trying to hurt me. Even if I am a terrible detective, I can't just sit here and accept it."

"I'm not saying let it go—I'm saying let the police do their jobs. You don't need to be the one who solves this."

Yes, I *do*. No matter what Matt said, someone had come after me. I couldn't just take that lying down. Well, figuratively anyway. For at least the next few days, I would be taking pretty much everything lying down since I couldn't put any weight on my leg. But I couldn't tell Matt that. Not right now anyway. Not until he'd calmed down a little.

"Okay," I said with a small smile. "I'll lay off. But if someone tries to come after me again, you better believe I'm taking them down!"

"Just smack 'em with your crutches." He gestured at Latte. "Or sic your vicious dog on him."

I looked at Latte on the floor next to the couch. He had fallen asleep and rolled over with his paws in the air. Vicious dog indeed.

Chapter Twenty

I spent most of the next few days on the couch. As the doctor had predicted, the day after my fall was worse than the day I actually got hurt. My knee was swollen and painful, and it hurt even worse when I so much as tried to get up to go to the bathroom. Keeping it elevated really did make a difference.

Matt took a few days off work to help me out and take care of Latte. I slowly gave up on trying to pay for the food that he either bought or brought over to cook. It was just too hard with my leg. Once I got back on my feet and was able to sneak over to restaurant cashiers, I'd start trying again.

Matt and I put together some Found Dog posters, and Matt drove us around town to hang them up. I got more and more used to having Latte around, and I hated to think about someone calling to say he belonged to them. I considered putting the wrong phone number on the signs but figured Matt would catch me. It was probably a good thing that I couldn't really get around too well, because otherwise I would have been seriously tempted to sneak around town and tear down all the signs.

Sammy held down the fort at the café. It would be a few weeks before I was really able to work normally. I called her every day to check on things, but she seemed to be doing well on her own. She mobilized our battery of part-timers to work the middle of the day and came in herself for open and close. I was glad my mother had trained her so well.

Still, I was itching to get back to my investigation. Every time Matt took me out, I kept my eyes peeled for men with canes. Whenever I saw someone, I'd make a note on my phone about who it was or what they looked like. I tried to pay particular attention to shoes and canes, since that was what I saw the day I fell, but it was hard to see those things when we were driving by. What I'd seen as I tried to catch my balance hadn't been that detailed anyway—just heavy black shoes and a brown wood cane with a black rubber bottom. Not exactly a unique or unusual combination. When Matt asked what I kept doing on my phone, I told him it was ideas for the café. I felt bad about lying to him, but I knew he'd have thoughts on the matter if I told him the truth. I didn't think he really believed me anyway.

My biggest problem was that I had so many names and descriptions of possible murder/tripping suspects and no way to narrow the list down. The only way I could think of to home in on the culprit was to figure out who had a connection to Mr. Cardosi. To do that, I needed Matt. But Matt didn't want me pursuing the investigation anymore. I had to figure out a way to get him to support my sleuthing. I probably spent as much time thinking about that as I did actually thinking about the case.

We were sitting in my living room one night as we'd gotten in the habit of doing—

him in my grandfather's chair, me on the couch with my leg propped up, Latte curled up on the floor next to me. It had been several days since my accident and several days since Matt and I had last discussed my investigation. It had also been several days since I'd heard anything from Mike about my assailant. I was beyond antsy.

As the TV show we were watching went to commercial, I heaved a big sigh. It seemed like an effective but subtle way to get Matt's attention without seeming as though that was what I was trying to do.

He sat up in his chair. "Are you okay? Is your leg okay? Do you need anything?" He had been that concerned and considerate since I got hurt.

"Yeah, I'm fine." I sighed.

"Then what's with the huffing and puffing?"

"It's just kind of frustrating that it's been almost a week and we haven't heard anything from Mike yet about who pushed me down the stairs."

"Investigations take time. Just think how I feel not knowing anything about who killed my dad."

"I know, I know." *If you'd just help me narrow down my suspects, maybe we wouldn't have to wait for Mike.* But I couldn't say that out loud. Instead I said, "I just keep seeing men with canes while we're out, and I can't help but think that one of them is the one who tripped me. Some of them I know, some of them I don't, but one of them was perfectly willing to kill me and may very well have killed your dad. How am I supposed to go about my life knowing that he could be planning to try to kill me again?"

"You want to start your investigation again, don't you?" I took a breath to answer him, but he barely paused before going on. "That's what you've been doing on your phone, isn't it? Taking notes about potential suspects?"

I nodded. Matt exhaled sharply but didn't say anything. The show we were watching came back on, but neither of us really paid any attention.

After a few minutes, Matt spoke. "Who do you have in mind?"

My heart pounded. I couldn't believe he was actually asking. This was such a good sign! "I only know a few of them."

"Who are they? Tell me the ones you know, and we can figure out the ones you don't know later."

I took a deep breath. "The ones I know: Don Sampson, Jack Newman, Paul Hamilton, Pete D'Angelo, Steve Baker, and Bill Stanton."

"How many do you have on your list that you don't know?"

"It's hard to say. If I didn't recognize them from day to day, I might have written them down twice or even more."

"Your best guess."

I picked up my phone and opened up the notepad app. I scanned my list and counted the descriptions I had entered. "About five. Maybe seven."

Matt nodded. He glanced out the window. "It's getting late."

My heart fell. I was sure he'd just been humoring me and was now going to make his escape.

"I don't think a lot of cane-users will be out walking around at this time of night. How about tomorrow we go drive around for a while and see who we can see? I've been around more the past few years, plus

I know a lot of people from the barbershop, so I'll probably recognize some people you don't know." He took a deep breath. "Sound like a plan?"

I tried to hold back my smile, but I didn't think I did a very good job. "Sounds like a plan."

"And what's your plan for once we have a complete list?"

"Then I need your help to figure out who had a connection to your dad."

Matt nodded. "You had this planned, didn't you? From the time you brought it up, your goal was to get me to help you figure out who else might be a suspect then narrow down the list based on who had a connection to my dad."

"Not quite," I said coyly.

"No?" he asked, a half smile creeping across his lips.

"I wanted your help with the connection to your dad. Helping me identify additional suspects is just a bonus." I was still trying hard not to smile too much, but Matt laughed out loud. I hadn't heard him laugh that loud or hard since I'd been back in town.

"Oh well, as long as you were only trying to use me a little bit!"

I giggled. "I wasn't trying to use you at all! I was trying to help you, and I just needed your help to do it!" I knew my logic wasn't quite sound, but we were both laughing so hard, I didn't think it mattered. It felt really good to just be happy with him.

Our laughter woke Latte. He stood and nudged my hand with his nose, then turned to stare at the door. For some reason, even though Matt was always the one to take Latte out, the dog still always came to me. It was as if he knew he was *my* dog, even when he had a helper in his care.

"Oh, come on, boy." Matt stood and patted his leg for Latte to follow him.

They went outside for a few minutes.

"Is there anything you need before I leave?" Matt asked when they came back in.

"No, I think I'm good," I replied, glancing around. My crutches were within reach, all the dishes had been put away, and there was nothing on the floor for me to trip over when I hobbled to bed. Latte and I had been sleeping in my grandparents' old bedroom so I didn't have to deal with the stairs.

"Well then, I'll see you tomorrow." He looked kind of awkward standing in the doorway, but I wasn't sure what to do or say to make him feel more comfortable.

I just nodded and smiled. "I'll see you tomorrow."

He went to the door. "You'll call if you need anything, right?"

He'd been staying at his dad's house so that he'd be close if I needed anything during the night. I'd been wondering if he was seriously considering selling his place and moving in next door, but I hadn't found the opportunity to ask yet, and I was a little afraid it would sound as if I was coming on to him. I liked the idea of him living so close by and didn't want to scare him off.

"Yes, I'll call," I assured him.

He said good night and headed home before I headed to bed with Latte trailing behind me.

Chapter Twenty-One

Matt came over in the morning to make us breakfast before we headed out on our mission. I hovered on my crutches in front of the coffee machine to make cappuccinos for us. It wasn't easy, but I couldn't very well let Matt do it when I was the one who ran a coffee shop. Matt made us pancakes. Apparently they were one of the few things Mr. Cardosi could make, so Matt ate them a lot growing up.

"It seems appropriate to eat them on the day we find my dad's killer," he declared.

"That seems optimistic." I only had a rough list, that we both knew was incomplete, of suspects, and we still had to figure out who on that list had a strong connection to Mr. Cardosi. Plus, I'd been wrong once already, and that made me trigger shy.

"I have to be optimistic." Matt shrugged. "I'm tired of waiting."

I understood the feeling, even if I wasn't as confident as he was that we would figure it out today. Even if we did, I wouldn't get my hopes up that we were right. If we found someone, they would just be a suspect, nothing more. I wasn't calling anyone else a murderer without some concrete proof.

After breakfast, Matt and I got in the car and drove around town. It was a beautiful day and still early, so lots of old folks were out taking their "morning constitutionals." I added a few more names to my list based on people Matt knew that I didn't or just didn't recognize. It simultaneously felt as if we were inching closer to finding the killer and moving further away. I knew that each name I added to the list might be the killer's, but also that if it wasn't, I was just making it harder to actually identify him. Still, I added them and tried to keep my spirits up.

As usual, a group of men was playing chess in the park. Matt and I recognized several of the men, but a few were unfamiliar, and two of them had canes. I considered chess players to be strong potential targets as I could easily have walked past them that day in the park without noticing if one of them was watching me. Playing chess with the men seemed like a good way to get information about the ones we didn't recognize without seeming strangely curious.

Matt parked out on the street and helped me climb out. Moving was getting easier as I got used to balancing my weight on only one leg, but I still got wobbly easily. He let Latte out of the backseat, because of course we'd brought him with us, and we headed over to the chess tables. Matt and I played each other the first game. He was terrible, and I made sure everyone knew.

"You're hopeless, Matt!" I said loudly. I heard a few of the men chuckle, and I looked around at them. "Do any of you want to play me? I can't handle winning that easily again!"

One able-bodied man stood. "I'll play you." He made his way to my table.

I didn't recognize him, but I figured it might still be a chance to learn some names. Matt walked over to the man's former partner, who I noticed with glee had a cane propped against his chair.

"Mind if I join you?" Matt asked the man.

"Not if you're as bad as she says." The man laughed.

Matt and I played a few games, moving to different partners each time. We easily got the names of all of the men with canes. Around lunch, we decided to head out to get something to eat. We went to Sandy's Seafood Shack again, because the lobster rolls were calling my name and they had a nice covered porch we could eat on with Latte.

"Do you want to keep driving around?" Matt asked as we ate.

"Maybe just a little, but I feel like we've found pretty much everyone we're going to find, you know? At this point, we've identified everyone who's out and about, so unless the Tripper is in hiding somewhere, we should have already gotten him."

"I need to go by the barbershop to pick up the mail. I was thinking I'd get as many of my dad's papers as I can, and we can start going through them. He kept track of all of his customers, so maybe we can find something there."

"Sounds like a plan," I replied.

We finished our delicious, buttery lobster and got back in the car. At the barbershop, I waited outside while Matt went in to get the papers. Getting in and out was too hard for me to bother with when Matt would only take a few minutes to get everything he needed. He came back with more than I was expecting—a big box full of stuff. He put it in the trunk and got back in the car.

"Did you take every piece of paper in the store?" I asked.

"No, just what was on my dad's desk."

"*All that* was on his desk?"

"It was pretty covered."

We set up shop with the papers at my kitchen table. It gave us plenty of space, and I could prop my leg up on one of the unused chairs. We started by sorting through the paperwork, arranging it all into piles based on category—ledgers, records, mail, things that should really have been thrown away a long time ago—then went through each pile, highlighting our Cane Walkers' names as we found them. It was a tedious process, and I didn't feel like we were actually making much progress. Almost every Cane Walker had gotten his hair cut at the barbershop, so it seemed like Mr. Cardosi had some level of connection to all of them.

Matt made us spaghetti Bolognese for dinner. He moved most of the papers off the table so that we had room to eat and didn't have to worry about splashing sauce on anything. We were both getting discouraged that we hadn't yet found a smoking gun, or empty cyanide caplet as the case may be, but neither of us wanted to admit it. I especially felt that Matt would be disappointed if we didn't at least find a new lead.

Matt cleared the table and washed the dishes as I continued through the paperwork.

"You know, I think my dad kept some of his records at the house," he said when he was done putting the dishes away. "Do you care if I run over there and see what I can find?"

"No, no, go. We should look at every available shred of evidence." I was glad he'd thought of more papers. We were getting toward the end of what we had, and I was a little anxious.

Matt brought my phone over to me in case I needed to call him. He let Latte out real quick, then he headed over to his dad's house. I kept flipping through papers. The mail pile was the only one I could reach, and it was phenomenally boring and useless. It seemed as if Mr. Cardosi had never thrown away a single credit card application or advertisement for business cards. Still, I had to look through everything. The one thing I needed might very well be hidden among all the junk mail.

My phone's text message alert sounded. It was from Matt.

Ran into Paul Hamilton. Started talking about Dad. Said they used to have coffee together, so I invited him in for a cup. Will be back in 30 minutes or so.

Paul Hamilton, the one who Karl worked for at the electronics shop, wasn't the most pleasant person, so I wouldn't complain about Matt not inviting him back to my house instead.

I continued flipping through the mail, finally landing on a section that seemed to be personal correspondence. I wasn't expecting to find anything useful, but it had to be more interesting than the junk I'd been looking at. It was mostly letters from

Mr. Cardosi's old military buddies and a few letters from family back in Italy. I skimmed each one then set it aside in a separate pile. They seemed like mementos that Matt might want.

I picked up one that looked as if it had been scribbled more quickly than the others. The writing was large and messy and missing the customary "Dear Gino" at the top. The contents were different too. No reminiscences of youthful exploits or updates on shared acquaintances. No, this one was angry. Aggressive.

Stay out of it, Cardosi! My finances are none of your business!

Directly beneath it was a response Mr. Cardosi had apparently written but never sent.

Paul, It is my business when you're using my name as part of your scheme. I'm not letting this go.

I looked at the paper, trying to figure out what it meant. Both notes seemed angry, but I wasn't sure if they were evidence. I flipped through the rest of the pile quickly to see if there were any more notes like them. There was nothing. I crossed my arms and stared at the kitchen wall. When I glanced back at the papers on the table, my eyes fell directly on Mr. Cardosi's note, and the very first word he had written. Paul.

Paul Hamilton walked with a cane. He said he used to have coffee with Mr. Cardosi. He was having coffee with Matt *now*. The cyanide that had killed Mr. Cardosi had been in a cup of coffee.

My blood ran cold. I grabbed my phone and dialed Matt. There was no answer. I had to get over there now. My crutches were across the room. I struggled up from my seat and hopped over to my crutches. I shoved them under my arms. Just before I started hobbling out of the house, I had the clarity of thought to put in a call to the police. I didn't know what I was walking into and didn't want to be trapped with a murderer with no help on the way. I dialed 9-1-1, pressed the phone between my ear and my shoulder, then started limping across the room. Walking on crutches was hard enough, but doing it while keeping my ear glued to my shoulder was next to impossible. I was inching my way down the front walk when the dispatcher answered.

"I need help. I need police now," I said into the phone.

"What address?" she asked.

I spouted off Mr. Cardosi's address, listened for her confirmation that she had heard it, then I let the phone drop to the ground. I could move faster without it. The distance from my house to Mr. Cardosi's seemed exponentially longer than it ever had. When I was a kid, I could run from door to door in less than thirty seconds. This would take me several minutes, minutes I didn't know that I had.

Latte seemed to know something was going on. He ran back and forth beside me, barking loudly the way he had the day I'd found him. When I turned onto Mr. Cardosi's walk, he went ballistic, running up to the door and punctuating his barking with long, loud howls. It was as if he knew the man who had tripped me was inside.

When I was just over an arm's length from the door, I lunged for it, turning the doorknob and pushing it open. Latte rushed past me and into the kitchen. I lost my balance and fell facefirst into the foyer.

"Matty, don't drink that!" I screamed.

I heard nothing from the kitchen. I was too late. I crawled, dragging myself into the house with just my arms.

"Franny?"

I looked up to see Matt in the kitchen doorway. I dropped my head to the floor in relief. He was alive.

He rushed over to me. "What are you doing?"

Matt started to help me up when I saw Paul Hamilton step out of the kitchen.

"I should have pushed you," he sneered.

Matt looked between Paul and me. "What? What's going on here?"

"Paul killed your father! I found letters between them! He was going to kill you too!"

"Franny, that's—" Matt stopped when he saw Paul moving across the living room, a look of pure hatred on his face.

Latte circled Paul, barking at ear-piercing volume.

"Damn dog!" Paul spat.

I screamed when I saw him lift his cane and strike Latte. Latte yelped and ran past me out of the house. I heard him barking and howling on the lawn. Paul moved closer. I wasn't sure what he was going to do. Matt was definitely bigger and stronger than him, but if the man would poison someone with cyanide, I wasn't sure I would put a poison-tipped cane past him either.

He swung the cane at Matt, and it came in too low for Matt to grab, smacking his shin. He grunted at the pain. Paul swung the cane again, striking my hand as I tried to catch it. Through Latte's howls, I heard sirens in the distance. We only had to hold Paul off for a few more minutes before the police arrived. Paul lifted the cane again as Matt moved to grab it from him. Before he could, Paul brought the cane down on the back of my head. I saw stars and, through them, the flashing red-and-blue lights of police cars.

Chapter Twenty-Two

Needless to say, Paul was arrested. When the police tested the coffee Matt had made for Paul and himself, they'd found enough cyanide to kill not just one but several men. Paul was charged with Mr. Cardosi's murder, attempted murder and assault for his attack on Matt, and assault for his multiple attacks on me. Just for those charges, he should be in jail longer than Karl had been, and for a man Paul's age, that was at least a life sentence.

It turned out Mike had suspected Paul for quite a while, but he hadn't been able to find any direct evidence to use to get an arrest warrant. Walking into a vicious cane-based assault on two people was more than enough to put him in jail while they investigated his motive for murder.

The police went through Mr. Cardosi's paperwork and found bills for clipper repairs that Paul had supposedly done for him. But Matt was able to show invoices and shipping documents that proved that Mr. Cardosi had always sent his clippers back to the manufacturer when they needed repair. According to Matt, he only trusted the people who had made them in the first place to fix them right.

When the police dug into Paul's books, they found that he had been recording electronics repairs for businesses all over town, repairs not a single one of them had ever ordered. When Karl started working for him, not knowing that the unpaid invoices were fake, he sent the ones with Mr. Cardosi's name on them over to him. Mr. Cardosi put two and two together and figured out that Paul was running an elaborate money-laundering scheme. He threatened to turn Paul in unless Paul did so himself. Apparently the money laundering didn't bother Mr. Cardosi as much as

Paul using Mr. Cardosi's name on the fake invoices.

The reason for the money-laundering scheme was every bit as crazy as the scheme itself, probably even more so. It had started with illegal betting on horse races. Paul was good at gambling—shockingly good—but that wasn't enough for him. He wanted to bet on the long shots. He started paying jockeys and trainers to fix the races. That had led to even bigger paydays and ultimately to the laundering scheme that was his downfall. It was pretty dramatic stuff for a sleepy little town like Cape Bay.

It seemed as though it took my leg forever to heal. According to the doctors, my fall into the Cardosi house's foyer had set me back a good week or two. Still, I finally got back on my feet (literally) and went back to work at the café. It was nice to get back into a routine again. I spent my time working, playing with Latte, and redecorating my house.

In a weird twist of fate, it turned out that Latte had actually briefly belonged to Paul—that was why he barked so much whenever Paul was around. Latte, whose previous name was Barkley, had belonged to a family that moved overseas for the father's job. They weren't able to take the dog with them, so they gave him to their neighbor Paul, who apparently seemed like a nice enough man. But Paul hit Barkley with his cane every time he did something remotely impish or dog-like. Paul quickly got tired of him, took him to the park, and let him go. Apparently Barkley disliked living with Paul enough that he never tried to go back. I felt as though Latte deserved a fresh start after his rough time with Paul and decided to keep him. I liked the name Latte much better than Barkley anyway.

Matt and I had been spending a lot of time together. I guess you could call it dating. We had dinner a couple of nights a week after I closed up the café and spent the day together at least once on the weekends. It was casual, but a lot of fun. And I had even managed to pay a time or two. It took me slipping the waiter my credit card on the way in, but I'd done it.

I was in the café late one quiet afternoon when Matt came in with a big smile.

"Hey! How are you?" I greeted him.

"I'm great!" He came around the counter to give me a hug.

I had to just lean into him because my gloved hands were all wet and slimy from the mozzarella I was making. "What's got you in such a good mood?"

"I sold the house!"

That was news that required a real hug. I peeled off my gloves and threw my arms around his neck. "Congratulations, neighbor!" I was excited. Matt had finally decided to sell his house and move into his dad's. It wasn't solely because of my presence two doors down, but I liked to think that I was at least part of his motivation. "This requires a celebratory coffee!"

I closed the lid on the mozzarella and put it aside before I turned to the espresso machine to steam the milk for our drinks.

"So I was thinking," he said, going back around the counter so he could face me as I worked. "I have to invest most of the profit from the sale of the house to avoid paying half of it in taxes, but there's a good bit of it I can keep."

"That's awesome!" I said, pulling the espresso. "Are you going to buy yourself something nice? A new car maybe?"

"Actually, I was thinking of taking a little trip. Maybe someplace exotic, like the Caribbean or Europe. Maybe even Italy."

"Oh, Italy! I'd love to go to Italy! I've always dreamed of seeing the place my grandparents came from." I poured the milk into the cup. It was silly, but I was making a smiley face. It was a simple, happy design for a happy day.

Matt smiled. "I had a feeling you might say that."

"So you just thought you'd try to make me jealous? Is that it?" I joked as I worked on the second cup, this one for me.

"Well, no. More like I thought you could come with me."

I looked at him, completely surprised. I had not expected him to say *that*.

"Yes? No? Only if I put us up in four-star hotels?"

"Um, yes, I mean, if you're sure. I don't want to take advantage—" I was stumbling over my words and had let the espresso sit too long to boot. It would be way too bitter to drink, so I dumped it and started over.

"You're not taking advantage. I want to do it. To thank you for everything you've done the past few months."

"Well, I didn't do all that much." This time I managed to add the milk to the espresso in time. I poured in a heart because it was simple and the cup was just for me.

"You were there when I needed you. That's all you needed to do."

"And I get to go to Italy as a reward?" I handed his cup to him across the counter.

"Yup." He looked at his cup then back at me with a smile and raised eyebrows. "A heart? You tryin' to tell me something, Franny?"

I looked at the cup in front of me. It was the smiley face I'd made for Matt. I was so flustered I'd given him the wrong one! "No, I meant to give you this one." I tried to hand the smiley face cup to him.

"Too late." He took a sip.

The bell over the door jingled, and a delivery man walked in with a large bouquet of red roses. "Francesca Amaro?" He came toward me.

"That's me," I said, glancing at Matt. He had an innocent expression that I didn't believe for a second. I signed for the delivery and set the roses on the counter. I pulled the card out and read it.

To Francesca. The beauty of these roses pales in comparison to yours. Signed, Your Secret Admirer.

"Really?" I asked, looking at Matt. "'Your Secret Admirer'? You invite me to go to Italy with you, but think you have to be coy with the flowers?"

"I didn't send them," Matt said.

"Sure, you didn't," I retorted.

"No, really. I would have sent you lilies. I know you like them better."

That was true. I did like lilies better. I looked in confusion at the card. "Then who sent them?"

"Damned if I know." Matt smiled. "But I'm the one going to Italy with you." He drank the rest of his coffee. "I've got to go. I have a travel agent to see." He leaned across the counter and kissed my cheek.

My heart fluttered a little. I would be happy to go to Italy with Matt.

"I'll see you later, okay?" he said.

"Okay." I smiled and watched as he left.

My life had changed a lot in the past few months, but it was all working out. I was home in Cape Bay where I belonged, doing what I loved, and planning a trip to Italy with the boy next door. Life was good. Very good.

Recipe 1: Dark Chocolate Cupcakes with Peanut Butter Filling

Makes 24 cupcakes

Ingredients:
- ¾ cup + 2 tbsp cocoa powder
- ½ cup boiling water
- 1 ¾ cup all-purpose flour
- 1 cup buttermilk
- 1 ¼ tsp baking soda
- ¼ baking powder
- ¼ tsp salt
- 1 ½ sticks + 3 tbsp unsalted butter, softened
- 1 ½ cups granulated sugar
- 2 large eggs, room temperature
- 1 tsp pure vanilla extract
- 1 cup creamy peanut butter

- 2/3 cup confectioners' sugar

- 1 cup heavy cream

- 8 ounces semi-sweet chocolate, chopped

Preheat oven to 350F. Line 24 muffin cups with paper liners. In a medium bowl, add cocoa powder and boiling water. Whisk into a smooth paste, then whisk in buttermilk until combined.

In another medium bowl, sift flour together with baking soda, baking powder and salt.

In a large bowl, beat 1 ½ sticks of butter with the granulated sugar with an electric beater for 3 minutes, or until light and fluffy. Beat in eggs and vanilla, then the dry ingredients in two batches.

Spoon batter into lined paper cups. Fill two-thirds. Bake for 20 minutes or until cupcakes are springy. Let cool in pan for 5 minutes, then transfer to wire racks to cool.

For filling:

In a medium bowl, beat peanut butter with 3 tablespoons of butter until creamy. Sift confectioners' sugar and beat together until light and fluffy, about 2 minutes. Spoon all of the peanut butter into a pastry bag with a ¼ star tip. Plunge tip in from the top of each cupcake to about ¾ -inch deep. Squeeze pastry bag to fill cupcake, withdrawing it slowly. Repeat for all the cupcakes.

For icing:

In a small saucepan, bring the heavy cream to a simmer. Add the semi-sweet chocolate to the cream. Let stand for 5 minutes, then whisk the melted chocolate into the cream until smooth. Let the chocolate icing stand until slightly cooled and thickened, about 15 minutes. Dip the top of each cupcake, letting excess drip back. Dip again and transfer them to racks. Using the remaining peanut butter filling into the pastry bag, pipe tiny rosettes on the top of the cupcakes.

Recipe 2: Snickerdoodle Cupcakes

Makes 24 cupcakes

Ingredients:

- 2 2/3 cups all-purpose flour
- 3 tsp baking powder
- 2 tsp ground cinnamon
- ½ tsp salt
- ¾ cup shortening
- 1 2/3 cups granulated sugar
- 5 large eggs
- 2 ½ tsp vanilla extract
- 1 ¼ cups milk
- 1 cup unsalted butter, softened
- 2 ½ cups powdered sugar
- 2 tsp vanilla extract
- 1 tbsp heavy whipping cream

- cinnamon-sugar (to sprinkle on top)

Preheat oven to 350F. Line 24 muffin cups with paper liners. Set aside.

In a medium bowl, mix flour, baking powder, 1 tsp of ground cinnamon and salt.

In a large bowl, beat shortening with mixer on medium speed for 30 seconds. Gradually add sugar. Add eggs, one at a time, beating well after each addition. Beat in vanilla extract.

Slowly add flour mixture and milk until just combined, being careful not to overmix.

Pour batter into liners, about ¾ full. Bake for 18-20 minutes or until toothpick inserted into center comes out clean. Let cool before frosting.

For frosting:

Mix butter on medium speed with an electric mixer for 30 second until smooth and creamy. Add powdered sugar, heavy whipping cream, ground cinnamon and vanilla extract. Increase to high speed and beat for 3 minutes. Add more cream if needed for spreading consistency.

Frost cupcakes with a piping bag or knife. Sprinkle cinnamon-sugar on top.

About the Author

Harper Lin is the USA TODAY bestselling author of 5 cozy mystery series, including *The Patisserie Mysteries* and *The Cape Bay Cafe Mysteries*.

When she's not reading or writing mysteries, she loves going to yoga classes, hiking, and hanging out with her family and friends.

www.HarperLin.com

Printed in Great Britain
by Amazon